D0450372

Illegal

Bettina Restrepo

KATHERINE TEGEN BOOKS
An Imprint of HarperCollinsPublishers

Katherine Tegen Books is an imprint of HarperCollins Publishers.

Library of Congress Cataloging-in-Publication Data
Restrepo, Bettina.
    Illegal / Bettina Restrepo.—1st ed.
        p.   cm.
    Summary: Nora, a fifteen-year-old Mexican girl, faces the challenges of being an illegal immigrant in Texas when she and her mother cross the border in search of Nora's father.
    ISBN 978-0-06-195342-2
    [1. Illegal aliens—Fiction. 2. Mexicans—Texas—Fiction.
3. Texas—Fiction.]   I. Title.
PZ7.R3245Il 2011   2010019451
[Fic]—dc22   CIP
                                                                    AC

Typography by Joel Tippie
11 12 13 14 15   LP/RRDB   10 9 8 7 6 5 4 3 2 1

First Edition

*For Manuela and Mimi—and the roots
you have given me*

WE ARE ALL IMMIGRANTS.

CONTENTS

Illegal

PROLOGUE

THREE YEARS EARLIER

"When will you be back?" I asked, holding Papa's hand at the bus stop.

Worry coated Papa's face. "As soon as I can earn enough money."

"Should I get a job too?" I asked. "I could see if they need help in the church."

Papa's eyebrows drew together over his glasses. "No. Your job is not to grow up until I get back." He cupped my chin in his hand and his eyes brimmed with tears.

I reached up and pulled off his glasses to clean

them with the edge of my cotton skirt. "Ignacio's papa never came back. Then her family left." What if that happened to us?

Mama shuffled her sandaled feet in the dusty road and cleared her throat. "Arturo, the bus will be here soon."

"Why can't we go with you?" I felt the dryness of the land crawling into my throat. "I promise I won't be a burden. Mama can stay here to take care of Grandma and the orchard. Please, don't go."

Mama smoothed the stray hairs from my braid. "Nora, we talked about this. You can't go with Papa. We all agreed this is for the best."

"I didn't agree. I don't even want presents for my birthday or a communion dress. We should just try harder. HERE!" I snapped at her.

Mama's face crinkled up in hurt. "It's not about wanting. Please don't make this so hard for him."

"I wish I could stay, but the buyers don't shop the pueblos anymore. The drought. No jobs. We need the money, *mija*." Papa pulled me close and kissed the top of my head. "I promise I'll be back. I always keep my promises." A small gold cross dangled out of his shirt. "I will. Even from far away," his voice vibrated.

"Do you really have to go away to make things better?" I asked.

The bus turned the corner and Papa released me, picking up his black plastic bag. I tangled my arms around his waist. "Don't go. Please, don't go. I need you, Papa."

Papa tried to separate us. "Nora, there is no other choice. This is how I will protect us. Just for a little while."

"NO!" I screamed. "NO! NO! NO!"

"I love you, Nora. *Te amo, Aurora.*"

Mama squeezed between us to hug Papa, but I found that I couldn't let go. Mama slowly wedged herself into my grasp, and he pulled away.

"Nooooo!" Mama's tight arms pulled me away and he boarded the bus.

I kicked and scratched at her. "We can't let him go. No, Papa, nooo!"

The bus lurched away, leaving me sitting in the dirt with tears streaking down my face.

CHAPTER 1
Mensajes

CEDULA, MEXICO

A promise.

Quinceañera.

A promise that we would be together on my fifteenth birthday.

I screamed into the trees. *"¡Mentiroso!"* A lone crow flapped his raven wings in protest. I adjusted the white barrettes on the sides of my head. Presents from Papa.

I was answered by the thud of an overripe grapefruit hitting the ground. Even the fruit couldn't keep their promises. It oozed into the dry dirt like roadkill.

Infestations. Not enough water. No buyers. I don't even know why we pick the last of the fruit just to watch it rot at the market. Things were going from bad to worse.

"You can't let it decay on the branch. Bad karma," lectured Grandma inside our concrete house.

"What if a buyer came and we didn't have the fruit? Then what?" said Mama.

The promises were becoming long, empty roads. No Papa. No money. No nothing. We knocked down the fence and sold the wood just to buy the fertilizer for the trees. Now, wild pigs rutted and chewed on the tender shoots that the bugs didn't gnaw up.

I crushed a few crickets hopping between the baskets, but winced at the crunching noise. I looked at my skinny bird legs and frowned at the scars. My heart felt like it had fallen asleep since my father had left. It tingled for a few months and then the burn began to spread throughout my body. I wished he would just come home.

He said all of this would be for a better life, but it seemed like things were getting worse. The school closed, killing my hopes that an education might be a way of fixing everything. Without some sort of plan, I would continue walking around in circles.

I punted the grapefruit like a *fútbol* and ruby red juice sprayed into the air like droplets of *sangre*.

A promise is just a lie you don't want to tell.

CHAPTER 2
Velas Malolientes

Our tiny two-bedroom house smoked like a *chimenea*, and our scarred wooden table looked like an altar. Grandma performed a ritual before we left for the market. She liked religion. One white candle for God. One red candle for Mary. One green and red for Guadalupe. A blue candle for Papa. A somber picture of Jesus hung next to a gilded cross whose paint had begun to peel. The woven rugs were worn from years of sliding around on the floors.

I looked at my cracked fingernails. How I wished

for nail polish instead of the crust of dirt I could never remove. Maybe even a pink glossy lipstick to cure my chapped lips.

"Hurry, light this pink candle." Grandma stood over several chipped ceramic bowls of hardening wax.

My eyes blurred as I lit the candle. "What is it?" I said, wrinkling my nose from the rancid smell. I noticed the dim light coming through the cracks in the wall near the foundation.

Grandma beamed like a full moon. "I have been experimenting with the fragrance of grapefruit. This is a scented candle I'm going to sell at the market."

The wick burned fast, and the smell of burned fruit filled the air. *"¡Que terrible!"*

Grandma swiped at the air, trying to move the smoke and smell outside the shabbily curtained window, but everything singed our eyes. "Get out!"

We coughed and sputtered. I dumped the candle into the trough of water just outside our door. The hot sizzle disappeared into the bottom of the rusty tin.

"I don't think you should sell those just yet," I said to Grandma.

"Well, maybe I could call them *Cazar de Espectro*. They could chase the bad spirits out of your house." Grandma imagined the best out of every situation. She'd probably tell people in the market this is a new scent from *Fabuloso*.

"Maybe you could sell it to kill the cockroaches," I joked. I noticed a large black monster skitter next to our door.

"You and that smart mouth." She pinched my cheek. "I was going to call it the Birthday Candle. You light it each year to bring freshness and light to your spirit."

The tingle in my heart flared up as an image of my father holding me while I blew out my birthday candles flashed in my mind. Three birthday wishes wasted on wishing him home.

"And the pink was for you." Grandma brushed dust from my shoulder. "So cockroaches are out."

Mama honked outside from the truck. "Time to go, we've only got an hour."

The truck used to be Papa's, but we sold it to Ignacio, the man who owns the land next to us. The money from the truck was paid to the *coyote* who took Papa away.

No pickers to help in the orchard. No truck to

6

drive—only to borrow. Our orchard was on its last legs. Next thing you know, Mama would begin to take the tin roof apart to pay the tax man.

I ran inside to extinguish the rest of the candles. My eyes burned, and not just from the stink. The smoky scent reminded me of Papa's shirt after a hard day in the orchard. Our family picture appeared through the gray smoke on top of the TV. Papa smiled at me, but I couldn't smile back.

A small mirror showed my reflection glaring at me. Full eyebrows arching across my forehead, high-lighting the deep part in my hair from the braid.

I had a strange feeling Papa was disappearing. I wanted something different for my life—to not be afraid, to have a future, to have my family.

I pulled the rubber band out of my hair and combed my fingers through the plaits, shaking my hair free.

I peered back into the reflection and swiped the tears away.

CHAPTER 3
Los Lentes

The unpaved road looked extra brown and burned and it was only April. Without the water from the Río Bravo, no one had enough irrigation.

The market was only a concrete block with a tin roof, but somehow it seemed ready to wilt from years of disrepair. A tattered blue tarp fluttered from the east side in the morning, and then moved to the west in the afternoon to keep out the scorching sun. I noticed the floors had been swept clean of the dirt, yet the spiderwebs in the corners still remained.

How could I get ahead here?

Each of the sellers had our plastic bins stacked with different fruits and vegetables. There was enough room to turn sideways between each stall. I wondered how their families survived, or were they slowly selling everything?

The Lievano family, who used to sell *cabrito*, now only sold a little bit of milk and cheese. I remember how Pablo cried when they had to sell his pet goat for the meat. Then, two years later, Pablo left for the border to work with one of his cousins. He said, "If South Texas can steal our water, then it shouldn't be a big deal for me to cross over."

The Gonzaleses only sold half the amount of vegetables the land could support because they didn't have enough water. They always talked about the governor making a canal system to send us water. We were lucky when the electricity wasn't out from the old power lines falling down.

Lolo's children ran in between the crates with their puffy cheeks and skinny pigtails. Lolo was getting even thinner because no one bought her candies or yarn. Sandra, a mere husk of a woman, weaved baskets with her eyes staring off in the distance. Santino put out some new straw hats in addition to his peppers, which could burn holes in your stomach. I wondered where he got extra money to buy the hats.

I opened the magazine I had received for Christmas—an American magazine that showed all things *quinceañera*. Beautiful girls wearing pink and white gowns. Embroidered elbow-length gloves. High heels that reached to the sky. Crowns to make any queen jealous. They were dreams printed on glossy paper.

A few customers walked around, but most were dreaming of what they wished they could buy. Lolo's daughters stared at my magazine and pointed to the girl's long earrings. I turned my back and buried my head in the pages.

I looked down at my tight jeans. It was time for bigger pants and a bra that wasn't a hand-me-down from Mama. But I couldn't ask for such things when we barely had enough to pay for groceries.

Tucked inside the magazine was my postcard from Houston. It had a map of Texas, a red boot, and a shiny silver star. Papa had sent it specifically to me. "I love you. I miss you," it said in a messy print. I wondered if he would even recognize me now.

One of Santino's new hats blew away in the hot breeze, and his profanity filled the air.

"Watch your mouth in here!" screamed Grandma. "Go light a candle for your sins."

Santino caught the hat and mouthed off to Grandma. "Who are you, the village priest?"

Grandma stood up. "Here is a candle. Go ask forgiveness in the church. You know better than to curse in front of children. What will the customers think?"

The vendors chuckled. There wasn't a single customer in sight. Santino took the candle and lit it next to his stall. Lolo's children made a funny face from the smell.

Grandma turned to me and whispered, "Sins never go unpunished. Always repent."

I giggled. Santino wouldn't sell a thing with the nasty candle burning.

Mama said, "Would you be a thoughtful girl and run to the bank for me?"

Masa cooked on a nearby grill. My mouth watered from the delicious smells. "Mama, what's for lunch?" I felt embarrassed for being hungry.

Mama fussed over the fruit to hide its brown spots. "We'll eat later. After the money comes."

I looked around. Tired women from other farms napped in their stalls. My stomach growled from the aroma of the burning grill. Grandma worked her

11

fingers up and down the beads of the rosary.

Mama moved the magazine away from my face. "If we don't get something today, we can't pay any bills or buy groceries." Her face turned red. "Please be my lucky star. You always make good things happen for us."

I shuffled down the street, kicking stones and avoiding the boarded-up store where the church had been. Occasionally people still lit candles on the doorstep.

The building glared at me. The nuns stopped coming, the church services and the school ceased. They were just more things disappearing from my life.

When would it stop?

CHAPTER 4
Banco de Nada

The bank, with its chrome and shiny glass, was the bright spot in town. It was the only modern building we had, with room for two shiny desks and chairs. A heavy safe sat in the corner next to one computer and a phone. It sparkled on our dingy street in an odd way. It just didn't seem to belong.

No one had enough money to keep at the bank, but it was the only way to *get* your money if you had family working in the United States. At least half of the men in our town, including Papa and the Lievano boys, had already left for the border. Soon the little boys playing in the doorway would disappear too.

The bell jingled as I walked through. *"¡Hola, Hector! ¿Cómo estás?"* I said.

Hector wore a navy striped tie. His short hair stuck out in six directions, refusing to obey all of the gel he used to slick it down. He was twenty years old and wore glasses like Papa. His wide face brightened into a smile. "Please tell me you want to open an account. The boss in Mexico City is begging me to open one account this month."

"Maybe we can fill out an application for Lolo's pig. Do we need to get the old sow a voter's card too?" I said, trying to be helpful. Hector gave me a dirty look.

No one was ever in the bank. The town was trickling down to a few families. One day they would be here, and the next, someone else owned their stuff and they were gone. There weren't any more girls my age, either. No buyers or sellers meant no money.

"Give me your glasses. They are a mess. You never clean them," I said, as cheerfully as I could. Hector pushed his wire frames in my direction. "Besides, no one in town has any money," I said while polishing the glasses. It felt good to talk to him, like the way I used to talk to Papa. I watched my callused thumbs rub the smudges away on the small wire frames with my shirtsleeve.

He pulled out his dusty paperwork. "If we don't get more remittances into this office, or even a few accounts, they'll close this bank and consolidate it to the next *pueblo*. We don't even have a stinking drug dealer in this town to spread the cash around. *Nada*."

Hector was right, but I hoped to one day have a fancy job like his rather than working for the rest of my life in the orchard, because picking was so boring. We would both be left to the fields and the white mesh bags of a picker. Sunburned, without hope, and full of bug bites. At one time I wanted to be a teacher. I could teach here in Cedula and never abandon my students.

"Did you watch the new Brazilian *telenovela* last night?" Hector asked.

Grandma bought a TV for us years ago when the citrus crop was better. "I wanted to, but Grandma likes to watch Mass at seven," I said.

Hector typed on his keyboard. "Ah, she can repent later."

Grandma never skipped Mass or any holy day. "You need to tell her. I'd be thrown out of the house for suggesting anything against God, especially a

15

telenovela." I thought Grandma's heart would break when the nuns stopped visiting our church.

Papa had missed the past three weeks of telegrams. I heard the *ping*, and the printer began to stutter out the paper. It was a telegram from Papa!

Hector peeled bills out into a large stack. "You're in luck. The money is here with a message." He clapped me on the back with enthusiasm.

I felt my sad smile dissolve as I rushed out the door. My focus tightened on Papa's note. I knew enough words to get by, but it was time to learn more if I wanted to go anywhere in life. My ambitions had to be tempered with my family's needs.

I'm sorry it is late. Tell Nora to be good. Work is difficult. Te amo para siempre y siempre, Arturo.

The computer didn't show any of his messy scrawls. I tried to remember his voice, but it seemed so faint that the absence of it made my heart sting.

A hot breeze pulsed through my hair, making me feel freer than I had in months. Maybe now would be a good time to ask for a pair of earrings.

When I delivered the stack of money, Mama squeezed my cheeks. "Thank you, *mija*. You are my

16

lucky charm." Mama passed the money to me. "Do we have enough?"

My heart pounded. "Enough for what?"

She shook her head. "Never mind. It will never be enough."

We.

The happy feeling crumbled, and I felt for my hair, gently pulling it back into a braid.

If we could be a "we" again with Papa, that would be enough for me.

CHAPTER 5
Tipo de Cambio

The money was gone faster than it had arrived.

Dreadful feelings in my stomach turned into hushed whispers in my head that I couldn't translate. It was like trying to listen to an argument through a wall. You can't hear the details, but you know it's not good.

There had been eight weeks of silence from Papa.

Angry. Uncomfortable. Nervous. I felt like that every day. I tried to escape to my trees, but the swirling feelings in my head only made me dizzy on the brittle branches. I braided and unbraided my hair again and again.

"Nora," Mama called. "I need you to go into town."

I lingered in the trees and pulled the last grapefruit off one of them. Our small farm was losing the last of its green. The trees were pressed closely together, but each branch clamored for water and fertilizer. I felt like I was watching my own little pets die because we couldn't afford to feed them. What could I do to help?

"Please!" Mama said in a way that made me feel guilty for not being more responsible. I couldn't dream in the trees forever. "I'll meet you at the market later."

I walked on the craggy dirt that had been pressed down from a few trucks traveling this path, yet brambles still insisted on growing and throwing themselves into the road. Tall pieces of ragweed mixed with burned-out remnants of cypress roots stood motionless in the ground from lack of rain. One string of electricity hung from a pole, swinging toward our farm. I carried a ripe grapefruit for Hector.

A raven cawed from the pole as if he were trying to send me a message.

Do *something.*

I shook it off. I felt like I had to apologize for all of the time I went to the bank to ask Hector for the money and nothing would show up in the computer.

I swallowed hard and tried to re-create our old patterns, although I felt like I was trying to put on clothes I had outgrown years ago. My reflection in the glossy door showed me a worried face and shabby clothes. My once bright orange shirt was now a washed-out tangerine with the armpits turning yellow and thin.

"Nora." Hector looked up from his computer screen. "*¿Qué mas?*"

We never asked the question on the tips of our tongues: "What is really wrong?"

Mama's frustration mounted each time I came back to report there was nothing from Papa. "Same things as always," I said, looking down at my shoes. Part of the heel was prying loose. "Is it here or what?"

"Don't act like a nasty little girl," Hector said hurtfully.

An uncomfortable silence filled the space between us. I noticed his glasses were full of smudges, yet I pulled my hands away and stuffed them deep into my pockets. His comment burned sharply into my pride. I felt my cheeks flush.

Hector pecked at his keyboard and softened his

tone. "You know, I look every day. I've even called the main office in the United States. Nora, he hasn't sent anything."

Shaking my head in refusal, I reached across the counter to look at the computer screen. "We have to figure out a way. I can't go home without something."

Hector crossed his arms. "I can't steal money for you."

"I'm not asking you to steal," I murmured, a rock in my stomach growing cold. "I have always been an honest person. I just can't wait around anymore."

Hector's mouth hung open for a second. "I'm sorry."

I stood in silence, waiting for some sort of explanation. "Where is he?"

The pain in my stomach began to churn, and a headache spread across my forehead. Suddenly I felt like I was going to faint.

Hector rushed to my side and gently placed me into a chair. "Just try to breathe. Let me get you some water."

I pushed my head into my hands. How would we pay for groceries this week? Or the taxes next month? This couldn't be real. The room slowly stopped spinning, but I heard a faint voice.

He's gone.

21

"What did you say?" I asked through squinted eyes. I needed to be stronger.

Hector patted my back. "It will be okay."

"No, before that. You said my father was gone. What do you mean by that?" I said, annoyed.

"What are you so angry about?" asked Hector.

"My father is not *gone!*" Venomous tones spewed out of my mouth. I took the grapefruit and hurled it against the steel safe. The fruit landed with a soft *goosh* and the juicy bits sprayed against the wall.

Hector pulled back as if I had slapped him. "What the hell are you doing? I'm your friend. If your family needs money, I have a—"

"No!" I shouted at him. "He's coming back!"

I ran down the dirt street while my head exploded with thoughts about Hector, my father's absence, and my mother's disappointment. When I passed by the door of the old church, I took a rock and threw it against the old wooden door.

I sat in the truck holding back the emotions. My throat tightened, making me gasp to keep the tears from falling down my face. I remembered when Papa got this Chevy. It was already five years old, but it was new to us—our first car. I didn't want my dreams to be flushed away just because we were broke.

22

Mama and Grandma pushed themselves into the cab of the truck as I looked away to hide my face.

"I need to pay the grocer. Then we will ask the tax man if we can pay in installments." She chattered on like I had a million dollars in my pocket.

Mama continued, "No more credit at the grocery store until I pay our old bills."

My breath came out in jagged bursts. It was all I could do to keep the tears from spilling out. Was this the end? Was this where we give up?

"Nora." Mama playfully tugged at my hair. "Did he send extra?"

"I can't," I said, hiding my wet eyes. I couldn't say the words.

Mama's face held such hope. "Did he send extra money?"

It felt like all of the air had been sucked out of the sky. I couldn't look her in the face. "He . . . he didn't send anything."

Mama slammed on the brakes and we all lurched forward. I could see the veins popping out of the back of her small hands. Her eyes flamed. "Where. Is. The. Money?" she roared.

I was gasping for breath from where the stick shift had gouged my stomach. Mama's disappointment

23

swelled. I felt myself getting smaller and smaller. Heat filled the car like an oven.

"The fruit isn't selling. The money is running out and where is your father?" she screamed.

I yelled back, "It's not my fault he's gone!"

Grandma yelled louder than both of us. "Please stop arguing!"

I flung open the truck door. "If I knew how to fix this, I would." The air ripped from my lungs.

I slammed the door and watched the truck rumble away in a cloud of dust.

I was worried about Papa. I had the empty feeling that he was gone from our lives forever. Why was Mama the only person allowed to be mad? And why did all of this seem to be my fault?

I screamed over and over again, but the vulgar words provided no relief to my breaking heart.

As I stumbled toward the orchard, I reached the first tree and threw up.

CHAPTER 6
La Voz

I had to do something to fix us before we burst into flame and floated away like singed paper. I sat on the highest branch, staring at the moon until the night air gave me a chill.

Go home, whispered the voice.

"Who's there?" I asked, but only the gentle creak of the trees answered me. I scratched at my ears and I almost lost my balance.

No one answered me. The voice was inside my head. It felt like the same voice from the bank. The same voice rumbling from my stomach.

The leaves shuddered as a crow tried to land and quickly took flight, seeing me in its roost.

Another sound echoed through the trees. Mama's voice was hoarse, like she had been crying. "Nora, come in!"

I heard the fight continue between Grandma and Mama. "How could you say those things? What does a teenager know?" It was easy to hear Grandma roar from the house.

From my tree, I saw Grandma stomping back and forth in front of the kitchen window. The more I heard the words, the more I couldn't control the tears coming from my eyes. I wanted to be stronger than my silly tears.

You know, it said again.

"She misses her father. She watches her crazy grandmother invent recipes to keep the fruit from rotting," said Grandma.

I leaned forward on the branch to get a better view of my grandmother pointing her index finger at Mama. "She doesn't have to know everything. Let her be selfish for once. Let her want for candy, a whole family, and a *quinceañera*. She is changing into a woman as we speak."

Mama yelled back. "Don't you think I know that? I see how the men in town look at her!"

Mama opened the screen door. "Nora! Come inside. We need to talk. Nora!"

I felt a shiver run down my spine. I could hear how she wanted to forgive me in her cracking voice.

Grandma's tone echoed angrily through the orchard like never before. "You don't have to take your frustration out on her."

Mama's voice stabbed back at Grandma. "How am I going to explain that Arturo might be gone for good? How am I going to explain to her that nothing is left?"

Papa couldn't be gone for good. I still had a scrap of hope. Something could be done. The ache in my heart made the voice stronger.

Find him.

Who was saying these things? Me? God?

Grandma interrupted Mama. "Is this everything to you? Money?"

I considered going back into the house, just so we could all stop screaming.

"Of course it's about money. How are we going to explain that this orchard and everything in it will soon be lost because we can't pay the taxes?" said Mama.

27

Grandma sighed. "Aurora, we need to pray. God can provide."

Believe.

Mama stood in the light with her hand to her forehead. "I don't know what to do anymore, and God isn't helping. Just look at this place!"

I knew what she meant. Cedula didn't hold hope for us anymore.

Go.

My heart jumped around in my chest. My stomach churned and I could taste the vomit rising to the back of my throat again. Lose the orchard? The voice made me doubt everything I knew and understood. I mean, why would God speak to me? What makes me so important?

"You don't think I'm fighting too?" said Grandma. "We own this orchard, but it's not everything. *¡Familia!* That is what comes first."

It was easier to pretend life was good and Papa was coming. It was more fun to climb through the trees than to look at the truth. I could just keep on being a stupid fruit picker and never think again. But I couldn't. I wanted more.

Mama stood at the door and called out, "Nora! I'm so sorry."

How can you move when the world is tumbling down around you? I was trying to stay a little girl, even though womanhood sprouted out of me in a new way every day.

Papa would want me to fix this. The voice echoed in my head.

Go.

I shifted my weight in the tree. The branch creaked under my dress. A few leaves crackled. The branch split before I could grab for another limb. I lost my grasp on the postcard. The darkness swirled around me as I tumbled backward out of the tree.

With a thump I hit the ground, and everything went blank.

CHAPTER 7
Aspirina y Aceite

I opened my eyes. It was dark outside but the over-head light shone dimly. I looked beyond the bed and into the mirror. The side of my cheek tinged purple and my lip was cut. My barrettes were gone. Although there was no blood on my face, plenty was splattered on the front of my dress.

"What happened?" I asked.

"Grandma and I were talking . . ."

"Arguing," spat Grandma.

Mama ignored her and turned toward me. "Out in

the dark we heard a huge crack and a thump. You screamed. We think the tree limb broke underneath you."

The falling. The fight. The voices. A large, pulsing bump grew from my cheek. I licked my lips and tasted oil.

"Aurora, we should take her to a doctor. Look at the size of that lump," said Grandma.

I didn't want to walk to the other village past Cedula where they had a doctor. "Who has been putting oil on my lips?" Mama pointed to Grandma.

"The doctor is a foolish old quack. He will tell us she only has bruises."

I remembered when I had an ear infection a few years back. This doctor prescribed aspirin and olive oil. When Papa had diarrhea from food poisoning—aspirin and olive oil. No real doctor in site.

"No, I'm fine," I lied. Grandma left the room in a huff.

Mama's face creased with worry. "I'm glad you're finally awake. You've been talking, but none of it made sense."

I noticed she was wearing the same shirt, but now it was streaked with my blood. "I don't want to fight like this anymore," I said, looking into her deep brown eyes.

31

Mama reached down and touched me gingerly. "I'm sorry about what I said. It was so wrong of me to explode and drive off like that."

I followed the voice from my head. "We have to do something."

Mama pulled me in. "I wish I knew what to do."

I burrowed my head into her shoulder until I felt the heavy puffs of deep sleep lulling me back to a fitful slumber. I awoke in the middle of the night, but I couldn't stay in bed any longer. The rest of the house was dark. Mama had curled herself away from me with my only sheet.

Stiffly, I pulled myself out of bed. The pain still lingered. The feeling of the voice remained. God spoke to people on television all the time, like on *telenovelas* when people are in comas going toward the light, or on some of those holy programs Grandma likes.

Are voices things people make up to feel better about their choices, or does someone really talk inside your head? Was the voice really telling me to go find Papa? How would I do it?

In the kitchen, I looked inside the money jar. We had enough to buy our way across the border, but then what?

A small light clicked on behind me. "What are you

doing?" asked Mama. Her eyes looked sleepily at the piles of money on the table.

"I was thinking about America. Do we have enough to get across?"

Mama rubbed the sleep out of her eyes. "I don't know."

I bit the inside of my lip. "I think we should go find Papa."

"I need some coffee." She yawned. "Maybe after the next harvest I could try to get a job in Mexico City and save more."

The answer became clear to me. "No. We need to go soon, not in a few months."

Mama shook her head. "We can't just leave. There are things to do, and we can't just leave Isabel."

"We're not leaving Grandma, because we would come back," I insisted. This would be the plan: find Papa, get some education, and come back to fix Cedula.

"Nora, we can't just leave. There isn't enough money," said Mama.

I felt my voice rising above our midnight whispers. "This isn't about money. It's about Papa and what we are supposed to do."

We wouldn't be abandoning Cedula. This would be the fix.

Mama looked at me with concern. "We can't just go."

Grandma stuck her head into the room. "What is all of this whispering?"

I poured water into the pot and lit the stove. "Mama and I are going to Texas to find Papa," I said with rising confidence.

She raised her eyebrows. "What? Are you crazy? It's five o'clock in the morning. Put the coffee away."

Mama shook her head slowly. "I've been thinking about it too."

I moved the stack of money and pulled out three mugs. "We're going to find Papa and bring him home."

Grandma crossed her arms. "We'll talk about this tomorrow. I'm going to call the doctor in the morning."

Mama and I said in unison, "No doctor!" Grandma stomped out of the room mumbling.

I handed the stack of pesos to Mama. "Take the money. Do it for us."

Mama's face was lined with worry. "Nora, I don't know how to do this. Maybe we should wait."

I pushed the money into her hands. "If we wait any longer, then we'll really be out of money."

I poured the steaming water into the cups and watched the lazy curls float upward. Maybe prayer was like steam, going upward to heaven. Then hopefully the answers rain back down when you need them most.

I pulled Mama's hand into mine. "We need to be a 'we' again. Then everything can be okay."

CHAPTER 8
Cartas

The word was frozen permanently into Grandma's face. No. No. No.

Mama eyed me with concern. Grandma stared off in a different direction, as if ignoring us would make the entire conversation disappear.

Later, I heard the voice from her morning Mass blast out of the television. Mama slipped quietly out the back door as I washed the dishes. The volume increased as the program continued, as if Grandma was trying to drown out her own thoughts with the television.

As I tried to sneak out the back door, Grandma called from the couch, "I forbid you from going."

"I'm just going out to the orchard," I called back to her.

"It's the end of the conversation. You are not going to *America*." She huffed air through her nose like an angry horse stomping in its stall.

I hesitated, because I knew how Grandma would react. "Mama went into town to buy our bus tickets to the border," I said.

Grandma gasped as if I had punched her in the stomach. "What! We have to stop her. That money was for the tax man."

"No, Grandma. I told her to do it." The cuts on my arm were still hot and red from the fall.

The rosary beads were wrapped around her hand so tightly I thought her circulation might be cut off. "God will bring Arturo back to us."

I didn't know how prayer would work. The harvest was finished, and nothing was planted for the summer. "We can't survive like this," I said.

"You can't go against God. I have to trust my faith," she said belligerently, turning back to the television.

"Where was God when Papa stopped calling? Where was faith when the nuns stopped coming to Cedula?" I asked, trying to trump her argument.

37

"Faith is believing when there is nothing to see. That's when God's plan is happening!" She yelled like I was deaf, trying to get me to understand.

What if faith was stupidity?

"God has been talking to me. He told me to go," I said back quietly.

Grandma rarely yelled at me. "Don't lie to get your way!" I backed away from her hand and the swinging beads.

"He's been trying to talk to me but I didn't want to listen. He wants me to find Papa." Was it really God's voice, or just my own trying to convince me?

Grandma pulled out the guilt card. "You can't. You can't leave me here alone."

I had my own stack of aces. "God told me to. You always preach that when God calls, you have to go. This is *my* faith."

My own stupidity.

She turned off the television. "You don't know God. You never went to church and you don't listen during Mass. You are a child!"

"Mary was fourteen when she conceived Jesus." I slammed the door on the way out to the orchard. "I'm old enough to know!"

I found my missing postcard leaning against a tree.

The trees always knew what I needed, and whispered stories in the soft wind. Maybe they were murmuring for me to stay? The dust swirled. I could still smell the faint aroma of fruit. The last few grapefruit hung like moons in the trees.

I climbed slowly into the tree's lower branches and sat. Leaning my head against them, I wondered deep down in my soul about the voice, and whether I was old enough to know anything.

Three mornings later, the sunrise stars above Cedula blinked like a sleepy baby waking from a nap. Grandma blessed everything again, including my shoes, and crossed me three times.

"I love you, Grandma. We'll be home soon," I said. I didn't know if that was the truth—because I wasn't coming back until I could fix things.

"Of course you will, *mija*." Her eyes welled with tears and she blessed Mama's luggage again. "But you can always stay."

"Don't cry, Grandma. I'll see you again."

Grandma stopped and took my face in her hands. "Of course you will. I will see you every day in the trees."

My heart shattered and the tears slid down our

faces. I wanted to feel her hands every day and to wake up and see the sun shining in her hair. How could I do this from so far away?

"Someday," I whispered. No words seemed good enough for this moment.

Maybe it was important we kept saying those things. It didn't matter that we didn't know what was going to happen. It only mattered that we wanted it. Maybe that is what prayer is for?

Mama twisted her hands and squirmed. "I'm sorry. We have to go," she said to Grandma.

I kept looking back. Long after I couldn't see her hands waving, I could still see her hair in the rising sun.

When we reached town, I imagined the tips of our trees waving in the mounting sun. I didn't have a postcard of Cedula. I would have grapefruit and the smell of soap.

Across the street, Hector jingled his keys to attract my attention. "Please, don't tell me you are leaving," he said with concern, pointing at the red suitcase.

I crossed the dusty road to look at him for the last time. "Make me a promise," I said. "Will you do me a favor and watch out for my grandmother?"

"Yes, of course." Hector searched my face, looking for answers.

The bus turned the corner with a heave. "Maybe you could watch TV with her? Or tell her when our money arrives?" I said quickly. "I need to know Grandma will be safe."

Mama motioned at me from across the street.

Hector kissed me on the forehead. "Be safe, my little friend. Until."

I cocked my forehead, "Until what?"

"Just until," he said with concern in his eyes.

I couldn't even form the words to say good-bye.

CHAPTER 9
Las Decisiónes

Outside of the Matamoras bus station, the stale air hit my face. The road oozed filth, and everything seemed to be dipped in a coat of garbage. Fear and excitement mixed in me like oil and water. Mama's hands were slick, but I held on to them anyway.

A young girl with liquid eyes looked through the crowd and locked eyes with me. She held out her hand. A beggar.

I had a few broken pieces of candy. "Take it." Her smudged fingers grabbed the bits of sugar.

"That was very kind, Nora," said Mama with a tight squeeze of my hand. "But be careful, we can't give something to every beggar."

I watched the little girl scamper away, and then she disappeared behind a taxi. A plastic Virgin of Guadalupe rested on the dashboard of the delapidated car. The idol wore a sad face and held handfuls of roses. The patron saint of the country I was abandoning. The deep eyes of Guadalupe stared at me. Perhaps she knew about my doubts. Maybe she knew the voice in my head telling me to go to America to find my father wasn't God's—it was mine. A dry gust of exhaust pushed against me, and I felt I had grown a million years since leaving Cedula this morning.

Mama pulled the address of the *coyote* out of her purse. "I guess we should find a taxi."

I waved at the taxi with the statue on the dashboard. "He seems safe," I said.

"My lucky girl. You'll help me make it through this," Mama said with hope.

The roads developed bumps and scars as we drove through the city. Horns honked as the smell of the exhaust choked me. Seeing broken telephones and run-down markets reminded me of what I was leaving and why. I laid my head on Mama's shoulder.

The taxi stopped next to the fruit docks. Wooden pallets, cardboard boxes, and random carcasses of citrus were scattered around the trucks. But here, there wasn't the lingering aroma of sweet fruit. It was the sharpness of diesel making my eyes water.

There was nothing beautiful about this place. Why would so many people come this way if it weren't worth the risk? This wasn't a choice or a whim.

We had to go and we had to survive.

No one ever talked about this part.

CHAPTER 10
Via

In front of my eyes, my plan shattered like a lightbulb on a tile floor. This produce depot reeked of rotting fruit, diesel, and danger.

The *coyote* approached us with a swagger. Shiny sunglasses covered his pockmarked face.

"How much?" I asked.

"Two thousand each." Tobacco stained his teeth, several of which were coated in silver.

"We don't have that much," I said, stepping in front of my mother, who had become mute. She trusted me. I had to do this right.

He licked his lips. "Then go back to your village, unless you want to pay with your virginity."

"Fifteen hundred. Nothing else." I tried not to shudder.

He grabbed the money. "I don't have time for you anyway. Get in the mango truck. It's leaving soon."

Trucks were roaring to life around us, dissolving our words into the dust.

We walked toward the cab of the truck, but the dockworker pointed to the back. "Inside the truck!"

He flung the suitcase in the back of the semi and motioned for us to jump in. The man on the dock made a low whistle and shook his head like this was a big joke. I wanted to spit in his direction, but my mouth had dried up in fear.

It wasn't *supposed* to happen like this. Shaking my head in protest, I watched my feet disobey me. I wondered if angels would watch over us on the way to America. I felt my courage shrinking.

We moved all the way to the back of the truck. The heat from the metal of the trailer pulsed from the late-afternoon sun. It seemed cooler in the direct sunlight than here in this oven.

There only existed a small space on a wooden pallet. "This is our home for the next ten hours," said

Mama, pointing to the floor.

A forklift crashed onto the truck, pushing more pallets in. The sound crunched around us as pieces of wood cracked against one another. A shriek escaped my mouth.

I tried to stifle my fear by clapping my hands over my mouth. "Mama, they're putting more stuff on the truck." Panic climbed from my chest and my skin grew cold despite the heat.

The curious dockworker smiled at me from the forklift. It was as if he knew all the secrets that no one was telling us. Fear was climbing my legs like heavy mud, ready to sink me to the bottom and smother the life out of me. "No, Mama. Let's do it another way." I shot up and pushed against the pallets looking for an escape. "Let's just ride the bus and explain to the people we are looking for Papa."

Mama pulled at me. "We can't; you gave him our money."

The noise from the machines was deafening inside the metal shell of the trailer. The air got heavier. The space filled up with the scent of ripe mangoes and heat. No crying or giving in to the fear. I had to concentrate on Papa. Our life could begin once we found him. I had to think clearly about our survival.

I took a deep breath to think. Food. Water. Money. Papa.

"We don't have anything to drink and we need water." It was also an excuse to get out into the air.

Mama pulled me down to our spot. "No, I'll do it. You stay here." She scrambled up and over the pallets, leaving me alone.

My body shook, so I closed my eyes in prayer, but words escaped my mind. The constant rumble made me rock back and forth, and waves of nausea hit me. I hated feeling like a cowering child who was hiding under the bed from the *chupacabra*.

I overheard the men on the dock talking. "The money is decent, but it would have been better if I could have found more to come on this trip," said one of the voices on the dock. Was it the *coyote*?

"The driver is always asking for more," said another voice outside of the truck.

I poked my head out of our space when the *coyote* saw me.

"*¿Chica? ¿Donde está su Mama?*" His teeth gleamed like a rabid dog I had seen once on the edge of Cedula before someone shot it. "Maybe I do have time for you today." He loosened his belt.

Pushing myself back, I growled, "Get back. You've

already been paid and I have a knife." My only weapon was my mouth and a few quick lies. "I'll cut you into pieces and feed you to a pig," I snarled. He pulled his lips into a sneer and walked away.

The air seemed wavy with the heat. My hand slipped through the cardboard of a mango box. I found a prayer card.

Many farmers pray over their crops, even dropping in cards like this one to bless future production. The only hope they have left is an unseen God who might save them from the poverty sitting around the next corner. I wondered where my God was.

On the front of the card was a somber face of Jesus, and on the back, a prayer in Spanish. A garland of roses lined the card where it said *Iglesia de Guadalupe*.

Mama climbed back into the truck with two gallons of bottled water. "It's all I could find." She touched my face, and pushed a strand of hair out of my eyes.

"Are you okay?" she asked with concern.

I reached back into the broken box and pulled out a mango. I placed the prayer card in my bra.

As I bit deeply into the soft skin of the mango, its yellow juice ran everywhere. I had to make a new plan. On the other side of Mexico, there stood a

49

new life to find. My father, education, money. These were things we needed to fix our situation.

I leaned my head against Mama's chest and heard her beating heart. I remembered how I used to hear Papa's heart too.

CHAPTER 11
Highway 59

Sweat covered my entire body. It ran down my back and soaked my underwear.

I jumped when the motor roared to life. It made the entire trailer growl. Mama's face pinched. It was hard to be courageous after all the events of the day.

The truck smelled funny, even with all of the mangoes. It reminded me of a wet, dirty dog.

The doors closed and I reached for Mama.

"La luz . . ." I whimpered. My body couldn't keep my fears locked in anymore.

But the doors clanked shut. A lock jingled. We were trapped.

"No, *mija*, there are no lights."

"Can't . . . breathe . . ." My chest ached with worry. I had never been afraid of the dark before.

Mama held me and rocked me back and forth. *"Calmate, calmate."*

This dark scared me in such a primal way. I wanted to scream, to run home to Grandma. In this nightmare, soon I would be falling, falling, falling.

The truck lurched forward, and the pallets slid closer.

Curling into a small ball next to Mama, I said, "I want to go home." The tears sprang from my eyes, crushing my throat.

She touched my head and rubbed my back in small circles.

"We're going home . . . home to Papa."

"Home . . . my home," I said into Mama's dress as the tears ran down my face. My breathing was getting faster, and I no longer felt in control of anything.

Mama reached for her rosary beads. I placed my hand over hers and we prayed until my breathing slowed down into shallow gasps. If Grandma was right, prayers could solve any problem.

Searching my mind for the voices I had heard

in Cedula, I imagined the dark eyes of the Virgin Guadalupe from the taxi. Maybe I could be brave like the man who saw her on the mountain? Maybe I could pray for her strength? Maybe roses would appear in the darkness as a sign we would be okay?

A real sign from God could explain our situation, but so far, none existed. Picturing Papa's face, I tried to remember his voice.

"Mama," I whispered, "I'm afraid I'm forgetting the little things about Papa. Like how he sounds, or which side he parts his hair on."

Mama sighed deeply. "You'll remember immediately when we see him. His hair flips over to the left side, just like yours."

I felt at my hairline. I had always tried to tug it to the right, and now I understood. He was part of me, all the way down to my hair.

"I wished we would have had more time on the telephone," said Mama. "He could have told us how to do this. But we won't have to worry about telephone times when we find your father. Everything will be better."

A big *thunk* of the truck and the darkness reminded me things couldn't be that easy. I tried to concentrate on good things, but a shallow memory of my last conversation with Papa floated through my brain.

I faintly remembered how tired he sounded. "We work from early in the morning until late in the evening. There is a new job on a huge building. This will mean lots of money for us," he said. The voice sounded clear, like he was talking in the next room.

But Mama pushed me away from the receiver. "But the taxes are late. The crop isn't doing well."

I stood closer to hear his voice. "There's so much work, and I only have two hands to do it all. If I had more hours in the day, I could make twice the money. If we work fast, this tall building should be finished soon. I'll never run out of work."

It seemed that Papa wasn't listening to the words Mama was saying.

"Papa!" I cried, but Mama patted me on the shoulder to be quiet.

"We're fine. The money you send helps us, but things aren't going so well. Maybe it's time I come to Texas?" asked Mama.

The phone made a beep and a mechanical voice said, *"Dos minutos."*

"Papa!" I yelled next to the telephone.

"*Mija*, don't yell. I can hear you," said Papa. "How is my baby girl?"

"Papa, I'm not a baby anymore. Could we come

to Texas this summer after the crop is finished?" My mind was emptying. I could only think about seeing him again and I couldn't remember all of the things I wanted to say, forgetting I was angry about his broken promises.

"Yes, soon my baby girl will be a woman. I promise we will see each other before your special birthday."

"Maybe I could come for a while and go to school? Even Grandma could come for a visit."

"No, *mija*, I don't know how yet. To save money, I'm always changing where I live. There is no address. But don't forget, I know where you are. You are in my heart, so you are never far away. I love you, but put your Mama back on the phone."

"Soon, Papa. Make it very soon."

And then a click. It seemed like time was always running out.

I didn't tell Papa I loved him. It would be the first thing I said when we found him.

The heat from the truck weighed me down. I tried to conjure more memories, but I was pulled into the present.

I tried to fill my lungs with breath, but only got a shallow gulp. "It's just so hot in here."

"I know. Have some water," Mama said faintly.

Drinking deeply, the lukewarm water splashed down my front. The prayer card melted into a pasty wet glob against my chest.

"Be careful, we only have so much. The driver will give us a break when we get across. *La migra* will check the truck at the border."

Later, when the doors opened, Mama's legs shook violently. I was convinced someone would hear her knees clicking like empty bottles. My mouth wished for more water, but Mama hadn't even had any. Fresh air circulated around the trailer and I wondered how long it would be until we had the break Mama promised.

"Mangoes. We're heading up to Houston," said the voice in English. Mama lay on the pallet with her eyes tightly shut. My eyes felt dry, but I couldn't seem to close them. I wanted to drink up the light for as long as possible before it disappeared.

"Load looks okay, but I have to look at your permits for the fruit," said the other voice. And then the door closed and my air disappeared.

Mama held me close and offered me water as my panic rose again. We prayed. I looked for roses in the darkness. I promised God I would go to church as often as possible.

The truck lurched forward. I could feel it picking up speed.

Mama leaned over to me and whispered, "We're in Texas. How do you like it?"

Her voice sounded rough. Her hands were shaking.

I wiped the sweat from my forehead. "I'm hot. Is there any more water?"

Mama's voice sounded weak in the dark. "Why don't you eat a mango?"

No more fruit. The smell tried to overpower me and the nausea was returning.

"I never want to eat another mango again. Ever."

Mama laughed a little. I could hear her voice getting raspy. She reached out in the dark and touched my forehead. "You're funny. We're almost out of water, and we have quite a ways to go. Why don't you rest?"

"Mama, you drink some of the water. You haven't had any." Mama worked too hard and rested too little. Once, I found her in the orchard, leaning under a grapefruit tree with bleeding hands. She had worked so hard her legs just gave out, and she fell out of the tree, nearly breaking her back.

"Don't worry about me, *mija*."

In the dark, the beads of the rosary clicked like knitting needles.

Putting my head in her lap, I closed my eyes only to be haunted by the weeping eyes of Guadalupe. My head pounded and the darkness swirled around me.

I awoke when Mama threw up in the corner. I had been leaning in the other corner because it was too hot to lie in her lap. Although my clothes were soaked, I had stopped sweating. The sides of the truck were getting cooler.

"Mama, are you okay?"

She groaned. "Don't worry about me."

"What's the matter?"

"I just feel sick."

Worry coursed through my body. Nothing seemed right anymore.

Mama's words blurred into the whirring of the truck.

"Mama, I saw roses in my dream. A real sign. The Virgin of Guadalupe is going to help us. God told me to come to Texas."

But Mama didn't move. I could only hear her faint voice.

She whispered over and over, "God, please . . ."

CHAPTER 12
The Lion and the Lamb

With a bounce, I jolted awake. Were we stopping? No. The truck lurched forward again and stopped.

It had been hours since we'd crossed the border. Only the numbing hum of the road singing, *ka-thunk. Ka-thunk. Ka-thunk.*

The truck driver was supposed to stop and give us air. Something to drink. He hadn't given us anything. My faith had completely disappeared. To hell with religion; I needed air.

Now only the stale smell of mango and our heated bodies filled the trailer.

I didn't know if it was my imagination, or my falling in and out of sleep. It seemed the world was getting smaller and darker.

Reaching for her in the dark, I touched her cold, clammy skin. "Mama, what's happening?"

Fear gripped me and I screamed, "Mama!"

She moaned like a sick animal.

"Are you okay?" I asked. I became afraid of death—hers or mine. Please don't let us rot here. This time, I didn't know exactly who I was asking.

"Uh, yes. No. I'm not sure. Maybe I should," said Mama. Her words ran together, not making any sense.

"I'm sorry." I rubbed her back. The truck went over a large bump and several of the pallets shifted toward us again.

The brakes squealed. "Mama, sit up. The pallets are moving." She leaned forward with more of a flop. Her shadowy figure seemed like a wet mop. Limp. Sticky.

"I think we are stopping. Maybe we're here?" asked Mama in a weak voice.

I hoped we were near the end of the truck ride. "Don't worry. We're almost there."

Then, with a loud *clink*, the door opened and light flooded in. My eyes stung from the bright rays of sunshine pouring into the semi.

Peeking from behind the pallets, I couldn't focus my eyes.

"Hey! We're here in Houston. Get out," the driver said in a gruff voice.

My vision blurred in the light. I looked down, squinting, and saw how gray Mama looked on the floor of the truck. I pressed my hand to my heart and felt the prayer card. "Guadalupe, give me strength," I prayed.

"Hey, I know you're back there. Come on. I gotta deliver this fruit around the corner, and I can't do it with you in here. Time to get your stuff and get moving."

This time, I stuck my head out to look at him in full view, *"Un minuto, por favor,"* I said in my most adult voice.

Mama looked at me. "Help me up." Her wrists seemed so tiny as I pulled her to her feet.

The pallets scraped and whined as he pushed on them. The driver banged the side of the truck. "Holy Jesus. What is that smell?" I could hear the anger in his voice. "What the hell did you two do in here?"

Mama struggled and swayed. Her eyes appeared cloudy as if she had floated away to some strange place.

The man glared at me square in the eye. "And who the hell are you?" he shouted.

I cowered back to Mama, but then remembered she was weak. I had to be the strong one. After all, I was the one with the vision of the Virgin—now was not the time to doubt myself. I felt adrenaline course through my body.

His tone irritated me. *"Nos estamos yendo,"* I said. I was determined to help us get away fast. Besides, didn't he owe us something for not stopping, not even once?

Trouble stirred in my stomach. The way he balled his fists. The glare of his eye.

He pointed at Mama. "Look, lady, it's one thing to be crazy enough to come this way, but I never would have agreed with having a girl back here."

His words sounded confusing, but I got the point that he was angry. Maybe he thought we cheated him? We were the ones who almost died. He was *supposed* to stop and give us air.

He glanced in the corner where Mama had vomited. I peed in the other corner halfway through the trip because there was a small crack. Although the pee was gone, the smell remained.

He pointed at us with a cruel finger. "Look, you

crazy wetbacks, I'm fixing to deliver this fruit to a grocery store. You want to ruin my load? You're gonna have to pay extra for all of this, and you definitely have to pay extra for her."

He continued to push into the truck. An opening cleared for us to escape.

With the sound of a threat, Mama's strength struggled to return. She cleared her throat. I pushed her and the suitcase toward the opening of the truck.

"¿Estaba tratando de matarnos?" My voice pitched like a wild dog. I found a bulge in the side of the suitcase. Grandma must have packed us one of her stink candles.

Mama could barely walk and I pulled frantically at the suitcase. The pallets tripped our every step. "Air! Water!" I pointed my finger at him, just to let him know that I was serious. How many times had I said this? I would not let this man continue his quest to kill us.

He sneered at my accusation. "Look kid, I don't know what they told you, but I always get paid something on this end. *No para.* Just be lucky you're here and I don't drop you in front of the police and tell them you stowed away in the back of the truck."

63

A word that sounded familiar. *Police*. He wanted to stop and call the police.

Worse than death would be the police. We could not go to jail.

Mama swore at the driver and stumbled. She melted stomach-first into a box of mangoes. I pulled at her wrist.

The trucker stuck out his hand and spoke to me in broken Spanish. "More *pesos*."

"No. No. No." I stood in front of the suitcase and slipped my hand into the pocket and around the candle.

I tried to remember the few English words Hector taught me. He practiced his words with the commercials from TV.

"*No para. No mas dinero.* No money." The money belt hidden around my waist felt like a concrete block. I made my legs obey the thoughts in my head. We had to get out of the truck fast.

The driver grabbed at Mama, but instead he got me. My hair stretched painfully away from my scalp. This was no school yard fight. I flailed my arms and absorbed the smell of his sweaty shirt until my feet left the ground. I was being pulled toward him over the boxes.

With my free hand, I threw the candle at him with all of my might. Without time to think, I turned and sunk my teeth into his arm until his salty blood ran down my chin. I pushed my arms with every ounce of my strength against his thumbs. Pain cleaved through my hands as I hit his face and throat over and over again.

All I could hear was Grandma's voice in my head. *Get them in the vulnerable spots. Without eyes, they cannot chase you.*

I grasped for the sockets and pushed my fingers in.

He jerked hard and the hair ripped from my head. My jaw tightened and he screamed. I squirmed out of his reach and out of the trailer.

He let go and clapped his own hands over his eyes. Bits of candle clung to the side of his head, and blood dripped from his chin onto the truck.

Mama squawked in a coarse voice, "If you don't want me to scream and act like a crazy woman, you'll stay away from us. I'll tell everyone you put my girl back here to kill me and steal her. That you were going to sell her to rich Americans as a *puta*."

Her words were useless against this monster and she still looked completely bewildered. He continued to moan as he pressed his hands to his face. Our declarations stood meaningless against his pain.

We staggered away from the truck. I grabbed Mama's hand and carried our suitcase with the other. There wasn't time to gloat over our victory.

A crowd of people formed across the street. They watched, but no one came to help. I had a strong suspicion this was not the first time they had seen a fight with a truck driver.

I turned in the opposite direction and pushed Mama to speed up her steps. I felt nothing except for the need to get far away from the truck.

The truck driver cursed while holding his eyes. "Damn stupid Mexicans! You'll never make it here. They'll deport you."

I turned around and did something I've never done before. I pointed my middle finger at him and kept walking. Fast.

I didn't know which way to go, so I followed the first things I could detect.

The smell of breakfast and the sound of distant church bells.

CHAPTER 13
Sanctuary

We walked in silence as I held Mama's elbow. Her breath pounded. I tried to keep her from weaving on the sidewalk like a drunkard. The terror of the fight dripped off us. This place was humid and full of concrete—like an alien world.

At a bus stop, we collapsed onto scarred benches.

"Where should we be going?" I asked. Grass grew in the cracks. The sidewalks bulged in lopsided angles. Writing was carved into the Plexiglas windows of the bus stop.

Mama stared into the distance. "Closer to the tall buildings. That's what your father talked about on the telephone. Tall buildings."

I hadn't bothered to look up over the trees in front of us. In the distance were the largest buildings I had ever seen. The windows winked in the sun. Was this the *Tejas* Papa had described?

Summoning my strength I said, "We need to rest and to find food." I could hear familiar music coming from around a corner. I recognized a word on the sign down the block: TAQUERÍA.

"Look. A restaurant. We'll go there and eat." We never had the money for a *taquería* in Cedula, but this felt familiar, like a sanctuary. A *washatería* next to the pink building shot out hot, stale air.

Mama stumbled over a crack in the sidewalk and crumpled to the ground. I helped her up but she felt like a limp noodle. "You are such a good daughter. Just wait until I tell your father how brave you are," said Mama.

The sun rose hot in the sky and the cement steamed in wavy heat patterns. My hands were still sticky from the mangos in the truck. Sweat beaded on Mama's upper lip.

"I can't wait to see him." I wanted to give her hope.

It would push us through. I felt like I was inventing lies that I would say over and over again, hoping they would become true. The voice in my head had fallen silent.

The *taquería* glowed pink and green. A blast of cool air hit me in the face when I opened the door. The tortillas smelled fresh and made me feel at home and a little safer. Everyone spoke Spanish. The music blared *Tejano* in a lively rhythm.

Mama placed her hand to my chest. "Nora, do you have blood on your shirt?"

I looked down to see the splotches. I tried to smooth the wrinkled cotton down, but rings of salt expanded around my waist in a rippled stain.

"A little. I think there's more on the driver. I bit him. Didn't you see?" The reality of the moment crept into my senses. I was doing my best to block out the pain, but the evidence stained my shirt.

"No, everything moved so fast, because he was screaming. You saved us."

I was growing braver. No thoughts, only actions. I wasn't waiting for someone to save us.

A waitress clunked icy glasses down on the table. The site of water brought me back to the present instantly. A busboy brought a plastic

69

bowl of chips and salsa.

"We didn't order this," I told the busboy frantically. "No extras."

"It comes with the meal," he said a bit snottily. I gave him an ugly stare.

We both grabbed the glasses. The cool water dissolved the cracks in my throat. Mama took deep drinks out of the orange plastic cup and I could hear her gulp across the table.

"You looked thirsty. *¿Tu quieres algo?*" asked the waitress. She wore a thick gold chain with the name Cecelia written on it. I couldn't pull my eyes away from her face and her dangling earrings.

Mama bobbed her head and her parched lips hung open like a hungry bird. "Yes, lots of water, and maybe a Coca-Cola for the *niña*."

I didn't bother to correct her. The ice in the glass felt good against my bruised chin, and a Coke would be nice.

"*Despacio*. There is enough water here for everyone." The waitress touched my head and smoothed my hair where the trucker had grabbed me. "You drink as much as you need, and I'll be sure to tell the busboy."

Mama smiled and reached across the table for my

hand. She looked better.

Outside the windows of the restaurant, teenagers strutted by in shorts and tiny tops. They almost looked naked. One of them had a star tattoo on her shoulder. They looked my age, but seemed so much older. Like a pack of feral dogs, roaming the outskirts of town until a meal appeared or someone shot them.

"She's nice," Mama said, gesturing to the waitress and ignoring my glances out the front window. "She knows how to give respect."

Nodding, I became lost in thought. Why would those girls dress that way? Did I need new clothes? Grandma said that only *putas* had tattoos. What did I know?

"I need to use the bathroom." I reached into the suitcase for something clean and not covered in blood. The shirt smelled like Grandma's hot iron. I wanted to hug it, to bring Grandma closer to me, but I worried someone might think I was crazy.

I pushed open the door to discover a half-naked girl bathing herself in the sink. Her deeply tanned back was emaciated and bruised around the edges.

"Shut the door, this ain't a peep show," she said to me as I stood in the doorway shocked and staring.

I slipped into the stall to escape her aggressive

stare. She looked like a naked version of the hunter girls, except without tattoos. I waited until I heard the door slam to come out, wishing I could tear off my old skin and flush away the memory of the fight.

The mirror reflected an angry red line that ran down my scalp from where the hair had been pulled from my head. I touched the hairline and rearranged it to the left, fluffing the hair out. I continued to wash until the water made me numb.

The dripping blood from my neck had stained my shirt. When I looked closer at the stain, I could see it.

A rose. The Virgin of Guadalupe's rose. She sent visions of roses.

It was a sign of strength. Not like a burning bush, or tears on a statue, or a mysterious voice in my head, but a real sign. I wondered if this counted as one of those miracles, like when a statue cried or Jesus showed up on someone's burned toast.

Was this God's way of talking to me? What if it was just a stain, not something meaningful? What if faith was just something a church made up to get money from villagers?

I needed to believe in something.

I pulled the shirt carefully over my head and folded it gently. The bloodstain would be my secret until I could figure out what was really going on.

There were plenty of signs in the bathroom. It looked like someone had gone crazy with a marker and scribbled everywhere. I couldn't even make out the words.

Mama switched places with me and headed to the bathroom. While she was gone, the food arrived. I saw the skinny girl sitting in a nearby booth. Her eyes followed people around the restaurant like a hungry tiger.

"Are you going to eat this all by yourself?" asked the waitress with the gold chain as she placed down our food. The waitress raised her painted eyebrows waiting for my answer. She looked over her shoulder at the kitchen, then sat down as if we were old friends. "What's with the bruise on your cheek?"

I answered her question with a question. This worked when a teacher pointed at you and you didn't know how to answer. "What's all that scribbling in the bathroom?"

"Oh, just graffiti from the gangs. I don't bother cleaning it anymore, because it's back up the following day."

"Gangs?" We didn't have any of those in Cedula. There wasn't much of anything to steal. A few people tried to grow *mota*, but it didn't do well in Cedula because of the drought. The drug dealers preferred villages that weren't starving. It's hard to sell drugs to people who can't even afford to buy a decent meal.

Cecelia gave me a warning. "Stay away from the gangs. Or is that bruise from one of them?"

Maybe those girls I saw were in a gang. The clothes they were wearing said nothing but trouble. "No."

A man across the room pointed to his coffee cup, and Cecelia rose from the table.

"Buen provecho," said Cecelia. She reached out to my cheek and pulled my chin up. "Was the fight worth the pain?"

So many questions and not enough answers. "I don't know. It was necessary." I couldn't reveal our problems to a stranger. What if she wanted to call the police, even out of pity? Were all Americans this nosy?

Cecelia patted my shoulder and moved on to the next booth to fill empty coffee cups.

The skinny girl rose as Cecelia walked by. "I can work just for tips and food. It will be good for both of us," said the girl.

"No, you can't. You aren't of age, and that isn't legal. Next thing, your brother would be dealing

74

drugs out of this place. I'm sorry, Flora, but you can't hang around here. You gotta go." Cecelia pointed at the door.

I looked away from the girl, because I had enough problems of my own.

Just like Mama said in Matamoras, I couldn't feed every beggar.

CHAPTER 14
Ponytails

Mexican pesos.

I approached Cecelia at the front register. "I have a problem." A tight feeling gripped my stomach, because it would be easy for the waitress to trick me and steal the money. She smiled with her golden teeth. Why would she help me when she couldn't help the skinny girl?

I held in my hand a few thousand pesos, what I thought would be the equivalent of the same meal in Mexico. It's not like we ate in restaurants in Cedula, either, so who knows if I was even close.

When in doubt, pretend that you know what you are doing. Grandma always whispered this to me when I was left alone at the market with the fruit.

"I don't have dollars—" I paused, grasping for confidence. "Yet."

Papa once told me to *look people in the eye.* The first one to look away is weaker, and you can dictate the price. "Can you tell me a place to make a fair exchange?" I asked. I had to sound like an adult.

Mama savored the word "fair." She avoided saying "best" or "final," because there was always a lower price than *best* or *final*, but a *fair* price, that was the deal you wanted.

Cecelia squeezed her lips into a fat smile, which made her eyes close. "*No problema.*"

I let out a sigh of relief. Everything had been so hard. All we had to do was find Papa. Or was it?

Cecelia wrinkled her forehead in concern and touched my cheek in kindness. "It's okay, you know. You're not the first person to arrive here like this," said Cecelia.

How did Cecelia know we'd just arrived? Was there a blinking sign on my forehead?

"I must see two or three people a month like you.

Hot, sweaty, tired. Like you've escaped a cage. My parents arrived by crossing the river in a wagon from Laredo. My mother almost drowned until my grandfather saved her by grabbing her ponytail and pulling her out of the water. Many people come this way." She told the story as if it were coming from a book.

I pulled my hand to my forehead. "We came hidden in the back of a truck. We're looking for my father. The truck driver fought us for more money."

"Don't worry about it." She pushed my hand with the pesos toward my pocket. "The meal is free. As for your papa, do you have any idea where he is?"

"No, we don't even have an address. No family here. Not even a place to stay." I realized that this entire trip had been my idea, and I didn't know what to do next.

"I thought this was going to be easier." We were lost and had no place to go. "We just want to find him and go home."

Cecelia offered a suggestion. "My cousin has some rooms to rent. It's not far from here. Safer than the streets or shelters."

"I need a fair price." There was that word again. "Fair." Not best. Not lowest. "We can pay, but it must be fair." I didn't even know what a fair price was.

I saw Mama's eyes flutter open at the table. Her cheeks had a warm glow, instead of the pallor of old, stale coffee, as we walked out into the hot air.

Grandma's voice echoed in my head. *When in doubt, start at home.*

As we walked out of the *taquería*, I took in the details all around us. The wooden apartments had better paint than in Mexico. More room existed between each building. Sprouts of grass tried to grow. I didn't see as many dogs eating garbage, either. Other than that, this place looked just like Mexico, except with newer cars.

I wondered how we would find Papa, because home would be where he was.

Here in the streets of Houston.

CHAPTER 15
Eye of the Beholder

Every part of me was hot. The trash by the curb smelled ripe, like a new version of stink candle. Even though our place in Cedula was falling apart, we kept it very clean. Neat and tidy made things feel safe. A flimsy screen door opened and out came a large woman in a flowered dress.

"Hola, ¿como estás?" said the woman extending her hand to my mother.

I stepped forward. *"Buenas tardes, señora. Cecelia sent me."*

"Yes, yes, of course," she said, turning to face me. "I'm Yolanda. I have a good place for you. One bed, a small kitchen with a table, and a *baño*. Sixty-five dollars a week. Rent is due on Sundays."

I peeked inside. The place smelled like someone had already been peeing inside, and not in a toilet. I tried to convince myself I had still done a good thing.

"We'll have an indoor bathroom?" Mama asked. Papa promised when he returned we would install indoor plumbing from a new well. Both ideas dried up in his absence.

"Yes, Mama," I said softly.

"The park is across the street. A nice place, full of people on the weekend. This is a great location," said Yolanda.

The empty park was dotted with picnic benches. In the distance sat a barbecue pit inside a pavilion.

I gave Mama a sideways glance, but she looked a bit dizzy. Perhaps we could find something better? It seemed like a lot of money, but she was in no condition to continue looking. I got us into this mess; it was my job to get us out. Besides, it shouldn't take that long to find Papa, and then we could leave.

A cool breeze came from nowhere and blew hair into my eyes. I took a deep breath. Salt. Brackish air floated from the park. How far away was the ocean? The trees rustled like a gentle giggle. I turned and saw large trees behind the building. They were larger than the grapefruit trees from our orchard and they waved a welcome hello.

I would just clean it up. I would show Mama how smart I really was.

"We'll take it for sixty," I said.

This was our new home. It didn't matter what it smelled like.

CHAPTER 16
Paper Products

Mama pulled the suitcase into the room and sniffed at the beds. Just as I thought she was about to complain, she collapsed onto a naked bed.

I flopped into the hard-back chair, but I felt the need to scrub. I wanted to erase the previous occupants. Grandma would have a complete heart attack if she knew we were staying in this filthy place.

Dim light spilled into the room from a dirty window. Mama looked older as she closed her eyes to rest. I felt drained myself and my head throbbed.

Something had changed me in the back of the truck. How many minutes had passed since I had left my bed in Cedula? Instead of the faint smell of mangoes, I could hear noisy trucks and smell hot garbage. I thought Texas would be a beautiful place; instead, it looked very much like Matamoras. Dirty. Smelly.

I watched a man pushing a cart full of soda cans. He had a long beard, and he was talking to himself. From across the street, he smelled like our apartment. Foul.

I let Mama sleep for a few hours while I walked around. Our street was named Quitman. On the next corner was a large plain building surrounded by a fence. I had never seen letters put together in that way. I wondered if "school" meant *escuela*.

Bright-colored playground equipment littered the yard. The windows hid under brown paper. Hope filled my chest. Papa always promised me I could go to school when we came to America. Maybe this was another sign. Why would God put a school so close to our new home if he didn't want me to go?

We were now in the future. The place where things could happen.

I tried to read every word I could see. I rolled them around my mouth like candy. Wherever I looked, there were words. Some I could understand; others I couldn't.

A neon sign blinked and flashed one block ahead. I could hear the loud music and see cars turning into the parking lot. As we approached, I could hear announcements in Spanish about a special in the bakery. *¡Bollios,* ten *para un* dollar! He mixed English and Spanish. I understood the Spanglish.

The cars in the parking lot looked as different as birds on a fence. Some were new and shiny. Some trucks had spinning hubcap wheels and writing on their rear windows. Children ran around chattering in Spanish. They ignored a car pulling out that screeched to a halt, almost hitting them. Their mother pushed a cart full of groceries. "*¡Niños! ¡Cuidado!*"

I missed the open market in Cedula where I knew the name of the man who roasted corn. The sweet smell of the smoke mingling with spices and the odor of older cars passing around the village. The smell of our fruit and Grandma's candles.

I shook off the homesick feeling and concentrated. Papa. We were here to find Papa. I couldn't tell who was Mexican and who was American. I wondered if we looked like we fit in.

As I walked into the produce section, I smelled mangoes and almost fainted. My stomach flipped over. Bile crept into my mouth.

I thought about Grandma. She would have loved to sell our grapefruit to this market. There was more food here in one section than we had in our entire market in Cedula. This was like her fruit fairy tale—magnified.

My strength returned as I walked toward the side of the store where a small office was labeled CAMBIO.

I went back to our apartment and woke Mama. "You have to see the neighborhood! A school and a market—with a bank inside." She followed me numbly down Quitman Street.

An older man behind the desk came and explained the rules for exchanging money. He wasn't as nice as Hector and was as ugly as sin, with long nose hair.

"There's a fee. Do you understand how to use American money? There are new coins, and bills mean different things."

I missed my friend and his woolen tie. I opened the wallet. "I understand." American money looked smaller than Mexican pesos.

"My lucky Nora," Mama said.

"Your exchange will equal nine hundred U.S. dollars."

The money in America felt like a lot less. The stack was definitely smaller. I think we had more money in Mexico. Now I truly missed Hector.

"Is this all? Shouldn't we have more?" I challenged.

He raised his eyebrows so that even more of the hair from his nose showed. "I didn't cheat you. I wouldn't steal from poor people."

I didn't know we were poor. I felt like the beggar outside of the bus depot.

Mama slanted forward and whispered to the clerk. "I also need to get a job."

He leaned in and lowered his voice. "I can arrange to have someone meet you outside tomorrow. She does good fake papers."

Her words shrank. "How much?" asked Mama.

"How much for what?" I asked, even louder.

"Only fifty dollars," he said, as if it was a bargain.

I didn't know what they were talking about.

Mama glowered. "Work papers."

"Ladies, talk about this outside." The clerk placed a CERRADO sign on the counter and went back to his desk.

Out of the corner of my eye, I saw a large pink cake being decorated in the bakery and the smell of buttercream floated toward me.

Behind the glass, a woman in white twirled the

layers in different directions. First a bright fuchsia trim, then a softer pink flower. On the fifth layer, she made soft swirls that looked like confetti and topped it with a sparkly crown.

I closed my eyes to seal in the moment. Pictures formed in my mind. The music in the market morphed into the band playing at my party. Grandma would be at the head table, near this cake, and Papa would be next to her. I would be wearing white gloves.

Find him.

The voice had returned to remind me to stop being selfish and continue looking.

CHAPTER 17
Wishing and Hoping

I couldn't get the clerk's words out of my head. *I wouldn't steal from poor people.* He didn't know anything about us. If Papa had been there, he would have yelled at him. Who is he to judge me? My emotions felt mixed up, like I was a Coke bottle shaken too hard, ready to explode on the first unsuspecting buyer.

Grandma taught me, *When something is wrong, clean until it's better.* "It smells like something *ha muerto*," I said, looking under the counter of our apartment. A dead rat lay in the corner, half rotten, melting.

I didn't even have the energy to scream. I stuck my hand into the plastic bag, scooped up the decaying creature, carried it to the large trash bin, and flung the tiny body away. A shiver ran down my spine, and suddenly tears sprung from my eyes. I couldn't stop shaking or crying. I would have to fight harder to make this work.

"Stop. Stop," I gasped to myself. But it all hit me. We had left. I was standing by a Dumpster. I didn't know where my father was. I didn't know anything. I was living in a place with rats, and I had almost died.

I covered my face and rubbed my eyes and tried to catch my breath, but I just felt so lost. I reached inward for a jagged deep breath and wiped my eyes and nose across my arm. I looked upward, trying to dry the tears out of my eyes in the hot sun.

Back inside, I scrubbed my hands and arms with purple *Fabuloso*. I even poured a little on the spot where I found the dead rat.

"I'm going out to the park," I called to Mama. She raised her head from the bed and nodded sleepily.

The shade loomed heavy in parts of the park, so that the grass had stopped growing. The crazy man pushed his cart in the opposite direction we had seen him go this morning, like he was returning from a long day of work.

I banished the dark thoughts from my head. It was only our first day, and I couldn't let my heart trick me into sadness. I observed a few houses with bars on the windows, but others had neat, green lawns and golden-orange marigolds lining the path.

In the park, I saw a father pushing a little girl on a swing. Her head tilted back as she squealed for him to push higher. I stared at them just long enough to realize that I couldn't recall the exact shape of my father's face. I only felt an intense longing and silent heartbreak.

A car passed by playing loud music. I felt like I was vibrating. Then it faded away, and the soft hum of the freeway danced in the streets.

I walked past a large statue of a cowboy on a bucking horse. A plaque had lots of words in English on it. The white cowboy had one hand flung in the air. The brown horse had an angry look and the cowboy tensed with concentration to stay in the saddle.

I decided I would be like him. I would hang on. I would tame my fear.

Up ahead, I saw splashing inside a gated area.

The water glowed blue like a clear sky, and kids were jumping and giggling. I could feel the droplets of water floating in the air as I stood watching. I could be one of those girls. Happy, with friends and clothes—with a complete family waiting at home.

Chapter 18
Legal or Not?

In the morning, we went back to the market and met the woman. She snapped her fingers as if we were dogs lingering next to a bush. "Hurry up."

"*Señora*, will these papers get me a job?" asked Mama.

"Where in Mexico are you from?" I asked.

"I'm *not* Mexican," the woman said, as if it were an insult. "I'm Colombian." Her Spanish was very fancy. She drawled out her words with a flamboyant *th* sound.

I didn't know where that was exactly, except they had great soap operas that were funny. Was Colombia south of Mexico? All I really knew was that Texas was north of Mexico. The world was much bigger than I had thought. But these are things I would know if I had gone to school.

She spoke so fast I could barely understand her Spanish. "Okay. We will take your picture and make several documents with a Social Security number."

"What do you mean?" asked Mama.

"You need a number to get a job and an ID," she said.

"I'll be needing papers also, so slow down," I said firmly.

This lady was acting as if she was doing *us* a favor. Her lipstick stained her teeth. It looked like she had blood in her mouth. "Never show these to the police or to someone you think really wants to see *real* papers. I don't give refunds. These papers are fakes, nothing more. To be honest, most people don't even care."

"The police don't care?" I asked.

"The police—they don't care about you or your problems. Just like me."

In Mexico, you also had to be careful of the police.

94

But who would protect us if something bad happened? Come to think of it, no one had come to help us as we fought to get off the truck. This is why we really had to find Papa—he was our protector.

Mama whined. "I'm just trying to find my husband."

The woman sneered at Mama with disdain. "Look, I just make the papers. You should have thought about that before you swam the river."

"We came on a truck," I said.

"Aren't you a fancy girl?" she said nastily to me, then turned to Mama. "Most people in this neighborhood don't care if you are legal or not. Just ask around for work."

"B-but . . . ," stammered Mama.

"And men are worthless. He's probably with a new girlfriend up here."

"Excuse me, aren't we paying you?" I challenged. "My papa wouldn't do that."

The woman stared at me venomously. "Do you want the papers or not?"

"We're not stupid," I shot back. "You don't have to treat us like this." Why did we need papers if no one cared if we were legal or not?

She began folding up the papers and putting them in her purse. "I don't need this. You're still wet from the river. Everyone will know you just came over, and it isn't my problem that you are so ignorant."

Mama reached out to her arm, pleading. "No, we need them. Please."

I pulled her back. "We don't have to beg."

She folded our money and put it into her bra.

I leaned forward as a warning that she wouldn't be leaving with our money. "I suggest you get us those papers." Her eyes moved from my face first. I had won. I fought the truck driver, and I wasn't afraid to fight her, either.

She clenched her jaw but pulled out the papers.

"Just take our pictures and we can be finished," I hissed at her.

"*Wetbacks,*" she muttered under her breath, as if we were low class.

I let it go, because some people have to have the last word. Papa used to tell me, *Know when the fight is finished.*

Outside, the crazy man parked himself on the corner. His sun-scarred face pointed into the traffic. I wondered when he stopped struggling and began sitting.

No matter what happened, I would always fight.

CHAPTER 19
Pounding the Pavement

"Papers. Cook. Clean?" It was hard to sleep with Mama mumbling all night long.

I elbowed her, and she turned over for the millionth time. We would never get any sleep if she kept this up. I would have slept on the floor, but I was afraid the cockroaches would climb into my hair. What I needed was Grandma's stink candle. Maybe it could scare away the huge flying bugs. But I had wasted it on the truck driver.

When the sun rose, I had to shake Mama awake. "It's time."

She rubbed her red puffy eyes. "*¿Qué?* What?"

I stared out the window and noticed the girl from the restaurant trying to get out of a blue car. She shook her head no, and then the driver slapped her. She fell to the ground. I noticed a large tattoo of a red star on his bulging arm with 713 underneath.

He got out of the car and as he was about to kick her, a scream escaped my lips. "No!"

They both looked in our direction. Fear coated the girl's face as she scrambled to her feet. The hulking boy moved in our direction, but the skinny girl held up her hands in surrender and picked up the green backpack. I saw a trickle of blood running down her nose.

Mama pulled me in the opposite direction. "It's not our business," she said quietly.

I turned away. But I felt even more horrible.

I needed a secret manual of how to make it work in Texas. It felt like everything was upside down and backward, but someone had to lead our way to Papa.

The furniture store appeared interesting. There was so much stuff, we could barely find the owner. Sofas smelled like the old men who played cards in the evening in Cedula. Papa and I would watch them and laugh as they told jokes and smoked. Grandma used to say they smelled like dust and farts. Either

98

way, my heart ached as much as my feet.

The bald owner pointed at me. "We'll take you. But your sister, no."

Mama stammered, "I'm her mother."

"Do you speak English?" he asked me in Spanish.

"I understand a lot. We could learn together," I suggested.

The man rubbed his head, and then his chin. "Try back next week."

He ran a chubby finger up my arm. "Unless you would like to do something today? Do you need some cash?"

A shudder shook my body. The taste of lumpy sour milk filled my mouth. He didn't want a worker for the store, and I wasn't selling what he wanted to buy. Hopefully I would never have to resort to what he wanted.

This went on for days. We asked everyone about Papa. We opened every door to every business we could find.

No work. No Papa. No nothing.

To keep my legs moving down the sidewalk, I thought about the times Grandma would wash my hair before Mass.

"Grandma, not so hard. I'm not that dirty." My hair

was getting long. I wanted to cut it, but Grandma thought I looked prettier with braids. Besides, I could do much better with a *quince* crown if I had long hair to weave through it.

"You must be clean for Mass tomorrow," said Grandma.

Grandma made me promise to go to confession. She's big on confession—sin and redemption. She would have made a good nun.

I wonder how many prayers I'll have to say to make this situation better? Or was I wasting my breath?

Hunger tore me away from my thoughts. The aroma of food floated from a lime green metal building. The woman working inside wore a tank top. Her hair was in a ponytail, and swingy silver earrings danced along with the rhythm while she cut vegetables. I pulled Mama in her direction.

I had a good feeling about her. "We're looking for work."

Her face was kind. "My husband needs someone for our stand by the pool." She looked at us the way you look at a lost dog. I didn't really like pity, but my feet hurt so much. I prayed silently for a miracle. Please God, no more walking.

"I'm Manuela. My husband and I have been running the stands here for eight years," she said, running a wet rag over the counter. "I haven't seen you around."

"We just moved here," I said quickly.

Then, with a cock of her eyebrow she asked, "Do you have papers?"

Mama dug into her purse and thrust them into the air. "Yes. We have papers." It sounded so rehearsed.

I came to the stand and looked up at the woman. She reached out her hand to me. The nails were short. She wore a silver ring on her middle finger that had red stones in it.

Her liquid eyes grew as she looked at me. Suddenly I felt shy and nervous.

I grasped her hand lightly. "You can trust us. We can work really hard. I'm Nora; this is my mother, Aurora." My words felt new and grown-up.

"Which school are you going to in the fall? Have you ever had a job?"

"No . . . I mean yes. I worked in our orchard, and then I sold the fruit at the market."

Around Manuela's neck hung a thin gold chain and locket. She touched it with her fingers. "Let me call my husband."

Mama held the papers to her chest. A broad grin

gripped her face. I stood tall and proud. Maybe this was our miracle.

Manuela continued to nod as a smile spread across her face. Her earrings danced and twinkled in the rays of sunshine. "Yes, I know. Tessa would have been her age . . . No, I'm not getting attached. They seem like a nice pair . . . just meet them and you'll see. She has eyes just like *Abuela*," whispered Manuela into the phone.

I tried to look like I wasn't listening, but I wanted to know the details. Who was Tessa?

"Do you know where Quitman Park is? That's where our other stand is located. My husband and I work both stands, but we want to open a restaurant. If you work with him, he'll have time to get other things done. Can you go and see him?"

"No problem," I said. "You won't be sorry!"

I wished I would have saved myself all of the walking and just looked in the park first for work.

Chapter 20
The Patron Saint of Liars

Even though the afternoon sun scorched the pavement, it seemed like my feet could move faster. With the money from my new job, I could buy new shoes. Leather, instead of cheap plastic.

At the park, we found the stand on the other side of the swimming pool. I hadn't seen it the other night when we were exploring. Children were buying *raspas* and potato chips. How could we have walked for days and missed what was right in front of us?

"Are you Jorge?" I asked the man standing behind the counter.

"Are you the women my wife called about?" asked the man over the giggling of the girls waiting for their Sno-Kones. Mama stood as silent as a rock, so I nodded my head.

"Then I'm Jorge," he said, jutting out his hand.

Mama shook his hand and I stood tall next to her. I noticed that I was almost taller than she was. It was our third day here. How could I have grown in three days?

The girls went back to the swimming pool. I could see the trails of water dripping from their suits as flies of envy bit my ankles.

"Tomorrow, be here by seven a.m. I'll pay you cash at the end of every day. Six dollars an hour."

Six dollars seemed like a lot of money, but I wasn't exactly sure how much bread it would buy or rent it would pay.

"Yes, that sounds very good," I said, "but if you want, we can start working now." I looked at the graffiti scribbled on the side of the cart. "I could scrub that off if you want."

His face told me something was wrong. I didn't want to lose the job. "Man, you look just like Tessa." He gasped.

"We live across the street, so there is not a problem. I don't think it would take me long to clean it," I said quickly, just in case he was wondering.

He put his hand to his chin. A small tattoo of a cross in between his thumb and first finger peeked out. "Our niece—you resemble our niece. No wonder Manuela was taken with you. Ah, Tessa." He sighed, looking away while shaking his head.

"This lady, Tessa—" I stammered, about to ask who or what she was. I didn't know what to do with my hands. What was I supposed to say? "I'm sorry about your loss." That's what Grandma would say whenever someone died in Cedula.

"Oh, she hasn't died, or at least we don't think so. She's just not *with us* anymore."

He shook his head and the moment was gone. "We do most of our business from the swimming pool. The city gives free lessons to kids in the neighborhood. In the morning and at lunchtime, we sell mostly to workers," said Jorge. "Don't worry about the graffiti. Just trash talk."

Mama cleared her throat. "So Nora and I will work here?"

"No. I think you should work with Manuela. I'll keep Nora here with me to sell at the pool."

I was glad to be near the swimming pool and in the shade. Maybe we would find Papa by working here in the stands. Papa had to eat, right?

Several kids screamed as they jumped off the board and into the crystal blue water. Splashes floated like tiny raindrops into the hot sky. I thought I noticed a green backpack.

Mama knocked me out of my daydream. "Señor Jorge asked you a question. Be polite to the new *jefe*."

"How old are you?" He looked me directly in the eyes.

It was a good thing I had spent an entire day thinking about this question. I would save my fifteenth year for when we were all together. It was supposed to be a magical time. It was mine to have, and I wouldn't give up my dreams just because things were a bit difficult.

"I'm sixteen," I said, as if it were the exact truth. Because it was—no more little girl.

Jorge's head was bald on the top, and the sides were filled with gray. His eyes were brown like Papa's. As he leaned down, I could see a cross on a chain hanging around his neck. It had the same red stones as Manuela's ring. "Okay, we're legal." Like a magician, he slapped his hands together as if he were showing us a rabbit had disappeared. With a wave of the arm and a few words—poof—we're legal.

"Last question," said Jorge. "Do you go to *la iglesia*?"

I noticed the crazy man jingling his cart toward the stand.

Mama stammered. I didn't know what to say. What was the answer he wanted? "We haven't found one yet," I said.

The crazy man parked his cart behind the stand and covered it with a tarp. Jorge didn't even look back, as if this happened every day.

"The church is one block past the Fiesta," he said, as if part instruction, part suggestion.

"We'll try to go to Mass soon." I felt like I had to say something with Mama turning into a statue at my side. "We usually just watched it on TV with Grandma."

"And where is your Grandma?" asked Jorge.

The dirty man disappeared with only a plastic bag.

"In Cedula," I said, looking Jorge in the eye.

"Mexico? I haven't heard of that town in ages. Such a tiny place."

It seemed like a tiny place now, compared to

107

Houston. It was small enough to sit in my head and burn a hole through my heart.

"Home is home," I said. Grandma used to say that.

We waved good-bye and went back to our apartment, which didn't feel like home at all.

CHAPTER 21
Mr. Mann

"Maybe we should try to go to Mass tomorrow," I said. "You know, to light a candle or something?" It's what Grandma would have done if she were nervous.

"Maybe another time." Mama rubbed her eyes and flopped onto the bed.

In the dark, the noise still crept through the walls. I held my postcard from Papa as I fell asleep. Houston was supposed to be my place of dreams. Papa's words rang in my head: *We will be together.*

109

Maybe it was a revelation. Maybe God was telling me to reunite my family. It says somewhere in the Bible that when a door closes, a window opens. Not that I had read the Bible, but the nuns told me. Maybe it's not God, but I'm going crazy. It echoed through my thoughts like music from a radio in a distant room.

Suddenly clouds came and thunder and lightning shook everything around me. Mama ran away. Grandma could not be found. Our house and orchard didn't exist anymore. I went through the entire journey of the truck by myself. Then I saw the crazy man and his shopping cart. Behind the cart sat Mama. When I approached, she didn't know who I was anymore. Then the hulking boy who hit the girl began to chase me down the street. I tried to scream but awoke to sweaty sheets and the sound of Mama in the shower.

I carefully wiped away the tears from my eyes and convinced myself everything was okay. Only little girls have nightmares, and I couldn't be one anymore.

Besides working in the orchard, I'd never had a real job.

"Mama, do you think we might see Papa today?"

Mama smiled into the mirror as she adjusted her dress. "Yes, let's pray for that today."

The neighborhood was just waking up and stretching. A few cars clattered by. A man slept in the doorway with garbage bags all around him and a dog tied to his bicycle. It wasn't the crazy man who parked his cart behind Jorge's stand. How many homeless people lived in this neighborhood?

We walked to the park and waited for Jorge as the sun peeked through the leaves in the trees.

"Ladies! How're you doing?" Jorge boomed, shattering the quiet. Birds fluttered from the trees.

He tossed a plastic bag in my direction. "Don't take this the wrong way, but Manuela found a bathing suit. She thought Nora might like to swim during her break in the afternoon." He held the suit out to my mother. The tags were attached. It was pure yellow, like the sun.

"Nora doesn't know how to swim," said Mama.

My heart sank. I wanted to be like the other girls. "I could learn," I said. The idea of making friends while lying next to the pool gave me hope. Mama nodded with a shy smile.

"First go to the truck and get the ice. I'll show your

111

mama how we get things ready in the morning," said Jorge.

The shadow of a man appeared from behind a tree and I shrieked.

Jorge looked up with a grin. "Good morning, Mr. Mann."

The man sneered at me and uncovered his metal cart. Jorge handed Mama a broom and continued as if nothing had happened.

I unpacked supplies and picked up garbage in front of the stand. I heaved several watermelons from the truck and placed them next to the cutting board. Mr. Mann never said a word as he clattered away.

I took the butcher knife and sank it deep into the watermelon's belly. Juice splashed out and coated my T-shirt. It cracked open, and the sweet meat spilled juice onto the counters.

I asked, "They really have swim lessons?"

"Yes." Jorge laughed at some private joke. "I'm always telling Manuela not to get too attached. I told her it was weird to go off buying a swimsuit for you."

Manuela arrived and Jorge lumbered out to her truck. She wore a different tank top, but the same earrings. He tugged at her ponytail. They hugged and kissed like newly married people deeply in love.

Jorge reached in and caressed Manuela's cheek, and I remembered when Papa used to do that to Mama.

CHAPTER 22
Lessons Learned

Jorge walked ahead of me to the pool and spoke in English to the lifeguard.

The blond girl sitting high up in the chair looked like an angel. Highlights in her hair twinkled like it had a lightbulb glowing through it. I couldn't see her eyes because she wore dark round sunglasses. I didn't see anyone my age except for one lone girl sitting under the trees, her face hidden in a magazine.

"Lifeguard," Jorge told me. I tried to get the words

to slow down, but I was only catching pieces. *Tacos. Swim. Free.*

I tugged at Jorge's shirt. *"Jorge. No entiendo."*

"Don't worry about Lauren," he said. "I have a deal with her that you can sell poolside as long as she gets free drinks."

The girl with the magazine peeked over the pages at me with curiosity. It was the skinny girl! Her cheek was tinged with a purplish green bruise.

Lauren raised her voice. "I don't speak Spanish. I don't know why they assign me to this pool."

Jorge huffed at her comments back at the stand. "Nora, your job is to come inside the pool every hour to sell snacks to the customers."

Jorge gave me a brown bag filled with a *torta* and a slice of watermelon. "Take this to Mr. Mann. He doesn't talk much and he's wary of strangers. Just set it a few paces from him and walk away."

"Who is he, exactly?" I asked.

"Just a homeless man, but he's still one of God's creatures. I let him park his shopping cart here because he can't take it inside the Salvation Army at night."

He sat at the corner. I set down the bag next to his plastic container of coins. He didn't make eye contact, and I didn't make conversation. When I

115

looked over my shoulder, he was already eating his sandwich.

The morning flew by. When I walked past the skinny girl, I noticed the bruises. *"¿Coca-Cola? ¿Galletas?"* I asked.

She examined my face and spoke with a sharp edge. "Lauren gets paid to do her job, and you can just do yours. She's not better than you."

"¿Qué? No hablo mucho Inglés," I said, trying to grasp her words, which overwhelmed me all at once.

"Time to learn," she said in Spanish. "You have to earn your own way here, and screaming across the park doesn't help no one."

"Me llamo Nora," I said apologetically. What could I have done?

"Flora," she said, ending our conversation.

By the time I looked up, it was the afternoon. Jorge tossed me the swimming suit. "Okay, kid. Time for your break."

He pointed to the locker rooms. "Go to the pool and make some friends. It's good for business. Be back in half an hour."

The yellow suit stretched across my body like a glove, but I felt shy about walking across the pool deck in something so revealing. Flora was still hun-

116

kered down by the shade trees and rarely ventured into the water. "Is this seat taken?" I asked Flora.

"Yeah," she said, without looking up.

I knew she was lying. "I've watched you all day; no one is sitting here."

Her painted eyebrows arched. "Who are you, a detective? Get lost, seat taken."

I gasped with surprise. My mouth just hung open.

"I'm sorry I couldn't do more," I said, lifting my feet back and forth. The concrete was getting hot, and I felt confused from her earlier words of advice. Was this her way of getting me back for all of those times I had looked away?

She glanced up at me again. "Jorge is watching. He wouldn't want you hanging out with me." She flopped her green backpack on the chair and shooed me away. "And what my brother does ain't your fault. Just move on."

I wandered to the shallow end and sat on the steps. I just wanted to wade into the cool blue water and disappear.

A small black girl with braids came through the gate and walked toward the shallow end. Each braid was fastened with a different colored rubber band. She looked younger than me.

Sitting next to me on the steps, she smiled broadly. "Are you taking lessons too?" Her hair was filled with beautiful plaits. "I'm Keisha. I can't swim real good, neither."

"Swim?" I said. I practiced the word because I had heard it so often this morning.

Keisha began talking. I didn't want her to get mad at me like everybody else, so I just nodded like I knew what she was saying. How old could she be? Eleven? Twelve?

"Hey, are we gonna start these lessons or what?" Keisha yelled at Lauren.

She pulled her sunglasses down her nose. "You've already flunked four times. Just stay in the shallow end and don't drown."

Keisha stood on the first step with the water. She splashed water around her legs and rattled on in English.

"Okay," I said, like I understood every word. *Pretend it's easy until it is.*

I liked the way her hair bounced as she talked. Her skin was so black it looked blue. Her suit was purple and little pieces of elastic were sticking out along the edges.

She kept saying the same words. "Swim." "Pool."

"Lessons." She pointed to the other end of the pool a lot, shaking her head. Did that mean we were supposed to stay on this side? I definitely needed to practice my English.

"Okay," I said again. I wasn't exactly sure what she was saying, but it sounded good enough. Flora watched us with interest, but never moved from her chair.

Keisha stepped in the pool and I dipped my feet in. I couldn't believe she thought I could speak English. It was nice to have a friend, even a young one, as the children in Cedula seemed to disappear with their families.

A chill went up the back of my knees. *"Frío,"* I whispered.

Keisha didn't notice me as she plunged into the water. The water reached up to her chest. It was so clear that I could see her feet touching the bottom.

Fear gripped my stomach. Something wasn't right.

But before I could retreat, I felt a hard shove. "Move it."

I heard Flora's voice in the background. *"Noooo!"*

I fell, face-first, and immediately swallowed water. My feet couldn't find the bottom. Swinging my arms made the water swallow me and everything slowed down. I felt a hand yanking on the straps of my suit. I was lifted up and water poured out of my mouth and nose. Keisha's hands pulled me to the side of the pool.

Lauren didn't move from her chair. She just sat there twirling her hair as two girls walked away cackling. They each had a red star on their shoulders.

My heart pounded. Why had I been pushed? At least Keisha saved me.

"Are you okay?" Keisha asked me. "Do you even know what I'm saying?" She said it louder, like I was deaf.

"She doesn't speak English, dummy," Flora said to Keisha.

My legs shook from so much pretending and nearly drowning. How could I learn quickly without being killed in the process?

"You don't speak English?" asked Keisha. "How come you kept nodding earlier like you understood everything?"

"Okay," I answered hoping the word fit into the conversation. Tears burned at my eyes and made my nose feel stuffy.

Keisha nodded as Flora strolled back toward the deep end. "I don't talk to Flora anyways. Her brother is a big gang-banger and those mean girls are also in a gang. I don't know why Flora is always at the pool but never talking to nobody."

How could this day get any worse? Nearly drowning, not being able to speak English, and even worse, almost crying in front of strangers.

But still, I wasn't going to let random girls bully me.

I closed my eyes and took a deep breath. Grandma would tell me to *try again*.

"Okay," I said again. "Swim." I slid off the side of the pool and into the water, but my hands remained glued to the edge. Keisha smiled as her rainbow braids floated in the water behind her like piñata streamers. Flora watched us carefully. As long as I could see both of them, things at the pool would be okay.

CHAPTER 23
Food

Park people trickled to the stand during my break. Most were sweaty in T-shirts and blue jeans, and I wondered what Papa was wearing. He left with four shirts, but I couldn't remember what any of them looked like. Watching people's backs as they walked away from the stand with bags full of tacos and tortillas, I wished Papa could see me swimming. Would he recognize me at all?

Jorge waved at me and pointed to his watch. I guess that meant my break was over. I grabbed

Keisha's arm and pulled her toward the stairs.

"Where we going?" asked Keisha.

"*¿Hambre? ¿Comida?*"

Keisha shook her head. I twisted my wrist in a circle like I was holding a fork and, moving it toward my mouth, made chewing noises and patted my stomach.

Finally she nodded her head yes to my game of charades. "Oh, we gonna get something to eat?"

I nodded. *Comida.* Food.

I knew Flora watched our every move, and I also knew she hadn't eaten anything all day.

Keisha put bright purple sandals on her feet. "You gotta watch out for the stickers, these little balls of needle weeds in the grass. Go put your sandals on."

I just shrugged and slipped on my old shoes. I didn't have fancy plastic ones like hers. I owned a single pair of shoes—the ones on my feet.

The concrete steamed beneath us and the sun cooked us and everything in the park. I didn't have a towel, and by the time we reached the stand, I felt dry.

I wanted Jorge to see how well I'd learned English. "Please eat for Keisha? *Ella es mi amiga.*"

"Hey!" exclaimed Jorge. "This food ain't for free."

123

But he piled two plates full and pointed to the picnic tables. Flora pretended she wasn't watching, but I saw her mouth twitch when the food was dished out.

"Is Jorge your uncle or something?" asked Keisha.

I told her what I thought she was asking. "Jorge. *Jefe*."

Keisha pointed a lot. Her eyebrows went up and down a lot as she talked. "Has anyone told you how much you look like his niece, Tessa? I just thought you was family and all."

She said the word "Tessa." Perhaps Keisha's chattering could help fill in the gaps of what I wanted and needed to know.

I nodded my head and put a tortilla in my mouth. Sometimes agreeing was the easiest thing to do, but I liked how she was herself. I wondered if I would ever be that comfortable in my own skin.

My shoulders felt hot. My skin burned red. "Tessa?" I asked in a hushed tone.

"You better put on some sunscreen. You gonna burn up," said Keisha, and then lowering her voice, "I'll tell you more later."

It had been many years since I had burned. Working in the orchard, Grandma made me wear long sleeves, a bandanna, and a hat. It never occurred to me I would burn.

"Sunscreen?" I asked. The word sounded funny, and I hoped I could get her to talk more.

"Cream. . . . You know, the stuff that keeps you from burning. You gotta get some cream and some sandals. You can't make it at the pool without that stuff."

Cream. *¿Crema?*

I didn't quite understand, but I knew I was red, and it hurt.

"I can share my stuff for a while since you bought me lunch." Keisha glanced at Jorge, then whispered again, like a juicy piece of gossip, "I never really hung out with Tessa. You know, once she got involved with the gangs."

Jorge interrupted and handed me a large plastic cup. "Break over. Give this to Lauren and do another round at the pool."

"It's time for me to go soon anyways," Keisha said sadly. "I hate swimming by myself."

I grabbed my basket and walked back to the pool with her. I put the cup under Lauren's stand and pointed. I didn't even bother to talk. She peered down from her seat, and slid her sunglasses back on her face and didn't say thank you.

I walked past Flora with the basket. "Are you gonna try to sell me something?"

"You didn't want anything the first three times I offered," I spat back at Flora.

"Girl, I'm just trying to help you out. Better get your defenses up before you get dragged down to the deep end. Swim now or drown later. I'll take a soda."

I took her dollar and handed her the soda. "Who are you, the lifeguard?"

She shook her head. "Yeah, in a way, I am. Go away now 'cause I ain't the library for all your questions."

I watched Keisha from the stand. She either stayed in the shallow end or sat under the trees reading. Occasionally, she looked at me and waved. I decided we were friends. When there were no customers, I tore a flimsy grocery bag into strips and twisted them into braids. Flora stayed in her spot and didn't leave until the pool closed.

My arms burned bright red, and my eyes felt like I'd rubbed sand into them when Mama returned with Manuela.

"How was your day?" asked Mama. Her hair was up in a ponytail, and sweat stained her shirt. Jorge counted money out at the truck as Manuela talked a

126

mile a minute about how well my mother had done at the stand.

"Good." I didn't tell her about the swimming part yet. "I worked really hard."

She looked so proud. "Me too."

"I bet we'll see Papa here this week."

Jorge interrupted by handing me two bills. "Nora, here's your money. Aurora, here's your money. We did very well today."

Manuela lightly touched my shoulder. "You've burned up today. Poor thing!" She reached out to hug me, but I flinched from the burn.

My brain swirled with thoughts: English, a new friend, and money. I tried to pay Jorge for the meal, but he wouldn't take a cent.

Flora emerged from the pool as Lauren locked the gate. She stared at me before turning her head in a different direction.

Mr. Mann clinked some cans together behind the stand, covered his cart, and disappeared into the afternoon shadows.

CHAPTER 24
Still Here

At home, Mama and I both fell into the bed. It smelled. We smelled.

I dreamed of Grandma's food. On long days in the orchard, I felt like this. Burned. Sweaty. Exhausted. I remembered how she made me a cold bath in the tub outside in the horse trough and I would sit in the water until it turned murky. After the bath, I would lie on the cool sheets of my bed and smell the breeze coming through the window. Grandma clanked pots in the kitchen and I could smell her love floating across the house.

Moist air-conditioning blew across the room, but it still felt warm. Yolanda told us not to open the windows. I wonder how many other people had lived in this apartment before us. Nothing but their broken dreams hung in the air, and they stunk.

In the bathroom, a large cockroach skittered down the drain when I turned on the light. It didn't surprise me. Papa had talked about how the big *cucarachas* were here in Texas. I decided to shower in the morning, and crawled into bed where sleep smothered me with nightmares.

"*Mija,* everything is bigger in Texas. The roads. The houses. The market. Even the cockroaches are bigger!" We waited three weeks to be able to talk to him the first time.

Don't go. Don't go. I heard it over and over again, like echoes in a canyon.

Then I could hear different voices. It sounded like everything was underwater. My mouth hurt, and my tongue felt as dry as sandpaper. I woke up with a shout. "Don't leave me!"

Yolanda pounded on our shared wall. "Quit your yelling!" She then turned up her television.

I moved outside to the steps of the porch. The rays of the setting sun danced away from the window. I used the twisty ties from the bread bags to secure the plastic braids into a small bowl. My stomach growled and my shoulders pulsed from the burn. We were still in Houston. I wanted to close my eyes and float back to my bedroom in Cedula.

One thought smoldered in my head: We'd never go back to Mexico now that we were here. I pushed it away from my brain by braiding small strands of my hair.

I woke up feeling like a piñata that had been covered with papier-mâché. Sticky. Stiff.

I had felt like this only once before. A large crop of grapefruits had come in from the trees and every hand was needed in the orchard. We couldn't stop picking and boxing and selling. That was before the water ran out in Cedula. That was before Papa talked about America. It was before the school closed.

Before. *Antes.*

Mama and I headed to the stand before the sun rose.

Standing by his truck, Jorge scratched at the bald part of his head. "I thought I bought limes. Nora, go buy some!" he said with a flick of the wrist.

I stopped by Mr. Mann with his morning sandwich. "I made you something for your coins." I placed the small plastic bowl by his feet, but he showed no emotion.

Inside the market, I bagged fifty of the best limes I could find. The evil mangoes smirked at me from behind a large display. Last night, I dreamed of fruit and hot trucks. I think I'd rather have cockroaches crawl through my hair than the nightmares.

At the end of the aisle, I noticed Flora holding a package of lipstick. Her hands slid down her sides and she put the packet into her pocket. She didn't see me watching as she walked toward the register and then past the manager, who gave her a funny stare. I glared at her from behind a display as she walked toward the front.

In church, they told us stealing was a mortal sin. Did Flora want to go to hell over a tube of lipstick? In Cedula, we heard stories about a boy who stole once at the market, and the owner sent him to the worst jail, and he didn't see his family for ten years.

I fell over the rack I was standing behind and the peanut packages scattered to the floor. The limes spilled out of their bag and rolled toward the check-out. The manager looked up from the desk and walked in my direction.

"I'm sorry. *Lo siento.*" I stuttered the apology over

131

and over again. I felt the blood rushing to my face. I grabbed the packages and tried to place them back onto the display. While I was picking up limes, I saw Flora slip a magazine into her backpack.

What if the market owner thought I was with Flora? Now I would be blamed for everything. The police would be called, I would lose my job, and I would be put in jail. We would be sent back without Papa.

I pulled the five-dollar bill out of my pocket and pushed it toward the manager. "I'm not stealing! I have money and I don't even know her." I was pointing at an empty magazine stand.

Flora was gone.

CHAPTER 25
Translation

When I walked by Mr. Mann, he mumbled at me. "Glad you're home, Tessa."

"I'm Nora," I said, alarmed by his voice.

His eyes rose in a flicker toward my face, but then quickly moved away. "It's spelled with two *N*s. M-A-N-N."

"Huh?" I said.

"M-A-N-N. They always spell it wrong." He lowered his head.

The pool opened at nine. The only person waiting

to go in was Flora. She sat in her regular seat by the trees, but wouldn't look at me. "Do you want your Coke now or later?" I asked, trying to read the cover of her magazine.

"I'll take it now," she said, handing me the dollar.

"Don't smear your new red lipstick on the can," I said. I heard the fizzing of the can overflowing when she opened it.

At lunch, I noticed a man leaning against the stand's tires—legs splayed, hat tipped back like a cocky cowboy.

"*¿Niña, tienes servilletas?*" He had soft brown eyes, and a dark tattoo peeked out from under his shirt. I handed him a napkin. His sunglasses were also smudgy.

"Thanks." Watermelon juice ran out from the corner of his mouth.

I felt my throat getting tight as I answered in English. "Welcome."

I worried about asking strangers for information, but I didn't want to wait for Papa to appear out of the sky. "Do you work on buildings? Tall buildings?" I gulped at my own courage.

"No. I work pouring concrete for new homes. They call me Concrete Guy because I'm hard to break." He chuckled at his joke. Concrete Guy wiped his mouth. "See you tomorrow, little one."

I figured it was silly to be scared of asking questions. If I had survived the ride, I could survive anything.

I walked around with my basket and Flora called out to me. "How much is a sandwich?" she said. "Or did you shake that up too?"

"Shut up," I said, embarrassed she figured out my little trick from the morning. "Don't you ever go home? If you stay out here all day, you're going to get skin cancer. The half sandwich is a dollar," I said to her.

Flora smirked at me with her freshly painted lips. "Is this advice coming from the girl who looks like a lobster?"

"Hey, I'm just saying you stay out here a long time. Why can't you act nice?"

"This is my version of nice," she said, her voice dripping with sarcasm. "And better to risk dying of skin cancer than to risk dying at home. I only have fifty cents, so I'll skip the sandwich."

Once again, she pulled her magazine in front of her eyes. It was the first time she revealed something of herself, and I knew what it was like to be hungry. I don't know why I did it, but I dropped a half sandwich in her lap. She tried to eat it without me looking.

Keisha arrived in the afternoon. "Girl, you look like barbecue." I saw Flora snicker—as if her version of honesty was better than mine.

I handed her a container of rice pudding. I saved it from my lunch. "For you."

Keisha's skin intrigued me, because I didn't know much about black people. Most people I knew were different shades of brown. Some like tea, others like coffee with milk. Never black. I hoped to touch her hair one day.

"Mama says I gotta pay something because I ain't supposed to be taking charity."

Jorge peered over the counter and joked, "Who said this was charity? Nora works for her meals fair and square. You're welcome to buy whatever you want."

Keisha had a dollar in her hand and she was waving it at Jorge. "She shouldn't be buying friendship with food. Some things just ain't right."

"Come on, girl." She looked at me. "You keep your pudding. You and me is friends without the food." Her words comforted me, even though they were foreign.

When I walked around the pool again, Flora turned

her chair away from our view.

"You want to swim with me at break?" I asked Flora as I walked by on my last round. "You don't have to sit by yourself all day."

"I don't swim with *Negros*. Go play with your little friend." Flora mouthed the word "nigger" at Keisha.

"I know what she's saying." Keisha looked hurt but raised her chin. "You ain't like that, right?"

My face burned a deeper shade of red. Why would Flora act that way? What had we done to her? No wonder people hate one another.

"You ain't gonna be friends with her, right? Don't be friends with a gang-banger wannabe," Keisha said loudly, trying to make a point.

We jumped into the shallow end. Her braids glistened with droplets of water. A sheen of color floated in the water next to her braids. But soon Jorge pointed to his watch and I was back to work.

What I didn't say was that for some crazy reason, I wanted Flora as a friend. She knew something about the world I didn't. But I couldn't just go along with the things she said or did. It was just plain wrong, and that didn't need translation. We all needed a little compassion.

"Hey, kid, watch the stand for a few minutes."

137

Jorge drove out of the park.

The sun melted into the oak trees. Keisha wandered toward the stand. "School will be starting soon," she said.

Something inside me broke open. "School?" I asked out loud. I grabbed both of her hands. "School? *¿Escuela?*"

"Eggs-squal-la?" Keisha raised her eyebrows. "You want to go to school? In the summer? On the weekend? Girl, I think you're nuts."

"No. School. I want school." I needed her to find the words in my mouth and say them aloud. Keisha was my translator.

"Look, school starts in a few weeks. We can get your mama to enroll you at my school. But you can't tell them about speaking Spanish and all. They'll put you in ESL, and I'll never get to hang out with you."

What was ESL? "I need to English." If I was smarter and spoke better, it would help me.

"Why? I don't get it." Keisha shook her head. My words didn't seem good enough.

"I school. No money. Papers."

Keisha nodded like she finally understood. "Don't worry. I don't have much paper either. Here they give vouchers for school supplies, 'cause my mom's a single parent and stuff. Maybe we can get you a voucher too."

"No. I no money," I tried to explain.

Keisha looked toward the curb as her mother's car approached. "Hey, this is America. You don't have to pay for school like in Mexico. We go for free. It ain't like charity."

Her mother honked the horn. "Don't worry, my mama don't like charity either. But she says if the government is giving it out like candy, you might as well use some of it. She knows how all of this works. See ya!" Keisha bounced away before I could ask the really important questions: What is charity, and how do I get some?

Flora sauntered up to the stand. "Don't sit out on the stoop at night."

"Who are you, my mother?" I gave back some of her medicine. "And don't call Keisha names, because she's a nice girl. A little girl who shouldn't be called names." I felt proud standing up for my friend. "And I'm just weaving. I'm not bugging anyone."

"Just sitting out attracts attention." Flora shook her head. "You don't know anything about this area or how this all works. The blacks live in a different neighborhood. They act different. They live different.

139

We don't mix. You shouldn't either."

"You're wrong. I may not know this neighborhood, but I know a good person." Flora shook her head, but I continued. "Why are you so hard on me?"

Her eyes were a misty gray, like the sky before an angry storm. "I'm just trying to give you some advice," she said sadly. "Don't act like Tessa."

"What do you mean?"

Jorge's truck sputtered into the parking space and Flora slunk away. "What am I? Encyclopedia Britannica? Ask your *jefe*."

Tessa was the ghost of the trailer. Hanging over our head and clinging to me like grease. "I'm asking you, since you know everything about everyone," I whispered loudly after Flora.

"She got involved with a gang-banger, got jumped in, and decided to get out. Then she disappeared."

"A banger? A jump? Like a terrorist with a bomb?" I asked.

"No, a gang-banger is a gang member out dealing and stealing. A jump-in is when you prove to the gang that you will be loyal. For a girl gang, you have to do ten or fifteen guys, then go through a fight with the girls."

"Who would want to do that?" I asked.

140

"Plenty of kids just aching to be part of any family," said Flora as she shook her head and walked away.

Mr. Mann clunked his way across the park. At the corner, someone threw a bag of trash at him. It exploded against his back and a river of soda dripped off his neck. Mr. Mann shook his hand in the air. I felt a wave of pity for him and set out lemonade.

He kicked it over and screamed, "Tell them to leave me alone. M-A-N-N!"

Shock rattled my body. Is this what I get for being nice? "They're not my friends," I shouted back, suddenly sorry.

He shuffled away violently shaking his head. "Tessa, when are you going to learn? Spell it right."

CHAPTER 26
Tough as Rock

The next morning, I noticed Flora sipping coffee at the bodega inside the market. She nodded her head at me in recognition.

"The pool isn't open for two hours," I said.

"Yeah, but my mom leaves for work at seven. I don't hang around because of my brother. He's kinda mad I won't do his . . . uh . . . deliveries."

"So, you just come here?" I asked.

"What's wrong with here?" she said.

"I'm buying the produce for the stand," I said, trying to prolong the conversation.

"Please don't stare when I . . . you know," said Flora.

The mention of the shoplifting made me uneasy.

She looked up and said quietly, "Thanks for the sandwich yesterday."

I shifted back and forth. "You're welcome."

Flora fidgeted in our awkward silence. "Cash is a bit short, so I'm just stretching things out. If you need something, I could get it for you." Her eyes pointed to the cosmetics aisle. "Like sunscreen."

I shook my head. "No."

She looked hurt. "You don't want to be around a person like me," she said acidly.

I walked away. I wanted a friend and I needed sunscreen. But stealing made the deal impossible. I would just have to figure out a solution.

On my way back to the stand, I dropped off Mr. Mann's breakfast.

"Thanks, Tessa," he grumbled.

"Nora," I said wistfully.

"M-A-N-N," he said back, as if it meant something meaningful. I noticed his coins were still in the plastic container, but my bowl sat next to it, empty.

My days began blurring together. Wake up, buy produce, sell tacos, swim, sell tacos, and go to bed. Wash. Rinse. Repeat. I stopped counting the days, as they all seemed the same. Full of work and empty of Papa. I needed to make something happen.

But today seemed different; Jorge wore dark jeans and a pressed shirt. He looked completely different from his shorts, T-shirt, and baseball cap uniform of the stand. Even his truck glowed from a fresh wash. "Nora, you handle things this morning. I'm signing the lease for our restaurant."

Halfway through the morning, Keisha showed up wearing a pink sundress instead of her worn swimsuit. "I wanted to see if you could come to Vacation Bible School with me. We get extra credit if we bring a friend, and I know how you like to craft."

There wasn't anyone but me. "Not today. Sorry," I said wistfully.

Keisha's shoulders slumped. "I've been telling everyone about you. Like hows we been good friends to each other, even though you a Mexican and all. It didn't matter about the extra credit and all." The car on the corner honked. "I gotta go, but I'll make you something in crafts. The teacher said I had a real creative side that I should explore."

I handed her a small tree I had made. "*Gracias*, Keisha." My heart followed her quick steps back to her mother's car. How I wanted to escape this hot trailer, full of burritos and chips, and follow her back to a simple childhood.

Out of the corner of my eye, I saw a man covered with tattoos swaggering up the sidewalk. *"Concrete Guy!"* I said.

"Little one." He tipped his hat, which was stained with sweat and grime. "Are you the *jefe* today? Where's Jorge?"

"He's getting ready for his restaurant."

"I'm glad. Jorge has helped everyone in the neighborhood. You and your mama must be his lucky charms, because every time they tried to open the restaurant before, it fell through."

Concrete Guy's hands were deeply lined. A jagged scar ran up his arm. "Where do men go to get construction jobs?" I asked.

"By the railroad tracks downtown where guys wait and trucks pick up," he said.

"I wonder if anyone down there knows my papa."

Concrete Guy raised his eyebrows in warning. "*Mija*, it's not a place for girls."

Concrete Guy rubbed his stomach, which made his tattoo dance along his arm. "I would like two tacos this morning. I'll miss Jorge's cooking while I'm gone, but *mi tía's* cooking is from heaven. I'm going home for a few days on the bus."

I saw another chance to get information, so I lumped extra watermelon onto his plate. "Would you mail a letter for me in Mexico?" I needed to stop waiting and make something happen to find Papa. I found a pad of paper under the register and tried to write quickly, but I couldn't spell every word I wanted to write. I wanted to explain how things had gone wrong and how I was lonely. I finished by saying, "I love you." Those words were the ones that mattered.

Concrete Guy folded the paper and put it in his pocket. "I'll mail it when I get across." He patted my arm to reassure me. "You're a good kid."

"I don't want you to steal," I said to Flora later at the pool.

"I just borrow. It doesn't cost the store nothing," she snapped back.

I shook my head. "No, really. It's a mortal sin and I wish you didn't have to."

"What, are you the Pope now?"

I chewed my lower lip. "You're better than that. You can work for money."

For once, her tough, cool exterior melted. Hurt

146

pooled in her eyes. "I can't work because I'm only fifteen. Not legal yet."

The words stung. This was her fifteenth year, and she seemed to be living day to day. I doubted anyone had given her a *quinceañera*, either. Seems weird how she was illegal, in a different way, but just like me.

"I need to know about Tessa," I said.

"She hung with my brother. He's somebody you don't want to know."

"Is that why you're here?" I asked.

"It's why I'm not anywhere. I'm just flying below the radar. You should too."

"Why does it matter what I do?"

Flora looked me straight in the eye. "'Cause I don't want you to disappear like her."

A shiver ran down my spine. I didn't want to be anything like this Tessa girl.

"I could have done something, but I didn't," Flora said with disgust at herself. "When she got jumped into the gang, my brother made me watch."

"What?" I said.

"It's a fight where you aren't allowed to defend yourself. Ten girls pummeled her. She never cried, she just turned her head and watched me like a dead

147

cat on the road," said Flora as if she were watching it replay in her mind.

"Why didn't you do anything?" I asked.

"She wasn't my friend. And what could I do? Save her from something she wanted? She got a new family. Getting into a gang is a way of being reborn. And being born ain't a pretty thing."

"Then what happened?" I asked, not really wanting to know.

"Those girls made it real hard on her because they wanted the power." Flora looked over my shoulder toward Jorge. "Just the sister gang. Some of them hook up, but the girls do their own thing 'cause they like the power and the drugs."

I thought about what that money meant. Death money. Dirty money. Money that strangles you.

"You don't want anything to do with it. Stay low and keep quiet." Flora pulled the magazine up over her eyes. "And it ain't stealing if I put the magazines back."

It was her way of acting tough. But I had learned that Flora was alone in the world. Kind of like me. "I guess this makes us friends now," I said.

Flora looked at me sadly. "I'm not really friend material, but if that's what you wanna call it . . ."

And I realized it was exactly what I wanted.

CHAPTER 27
July

Flora had disappeared from the pool for several days after our last conversation.

"Where have you been?" I asked with a sour tone. It had been three days.

"Things have been a little tough at home," she said. "I'm not taking stuff anymore, but don't think it was anything you said."

I smiled to myself because I knew it was *exactly* because of what I had said.

She twisted her mouth. "I'm not in a gang. My

149

brother pays the bills my mom's job doesn't." She took a deep breath. "I kinda wish my brother would get capped; then I could be done—just go home and be normal. But without him, the bills wouldn't get paid."

I noticed she looked even thinner. Her hair usually covered up her shoulders, but they seemed to be jutting out more than usual. "Are you hungry?" I asked.

Her eyes looked tired. "Yeah, I haven't been home in a few days."

"Is your mother worried?" I asked, giving her a plate of leftover fajitas.

"Nope. I don't think she even knew I was gone. You're lucky with your mother—how she's always looking out for you."

Mama was trying hard, but lots of times I felt very alone.

"When I'm seventeen, I'm out of this neighborhood. I still got a chance of being something more than this, so maybe I'll join the military."

"Where's your father?" I asked. "Could he help out?" I thought about how Papa was so much of my life, even in his absence.

"Nope. Gone." She said it like he never existed.

"So what are you going to do?" I asked.

"What am I supposed to do? Crafts at the Boys and

Girls Club? I got the pool and I got a bed. Occasionally, I got the library when things go really bad."

I looked at her hands. "You painted your nails," I said.

Her eyes brightened as she opened her green backpack. "Yeah, I got like six bottles of polish. The lady was throwing them away because they were expired. How can nail polish go bad?"

I shrugged my shoulders, but stared at the glossy pink with sparkles.

"You want me to paint yours?" Flora said between hasty bites of fajitas.

"I've never had my fingernails painted. Could you do it in the pink?"

She held my hand so that my fingers dangled. I noticed the beginnings of a star tattoo between her thumb and first finger. "What's that?" I asked.

She grabbed my other hand and began painting my nails. "Something I ain't gonna finish."

If it was possible, the days grew hotter. The blue water of the pool looked like a heavy soup with people of every color splashing in and out.

Flora sat under the trees, looking hollow until the stand would empty of customers. She would come over and repaint my nails or braid my hair. I would do the same for her. I fed her the old sandwiches we usually threw away while we painted and repainted our toes with the nail polish. We talked, but never about the things we really wanted to say.

I questioned more workers as they came to the stand. "Do you know an Arturo Mirales? He works construction."

No one knew my papa. It seemed we were doing more working than looking. I missed Grandma terribly. I didn't talk to Flora about that, either.

Even my dreams felt tired and humid. How could I have a *quinceañera* if I felt a thousand years old?

I needed to make something happen instead of waiting for the information to float into Quitman Park. At the apartment, I sat on the stoop, thinking of what life could be if I just had an education.

Mama walked up the sidewalk and sat down next to me. "Where has your friend, the little black girl, gone?"

I sighed. "She went to Vacation Bible School. She wanted me to come with her, but I said I had to work."

"You didn't tell her anything, did you?" asked Mama with concern.

"What would I tell her? She's not going to call *la*

migra." I felt my hands go up to my hair to try to comb out the tangles.

"I hear the other girl is a troublemaker," said Mama, jingling coins in her pocket.

I paused, curling my fingers under my legs. "Not true," I said. I gave Flora a little bit of free food, but I didn't consider feeding the poor anywhere close to stealing.

"Just remember, you can't feed every beggar." Mama ruffled my hair. "I got a phone number today from someone who really described Papa."

"What are we sitting here for? Let's go!" I said. We ran down to the market where we would wait in line with the others to use the public phone.

Even though it was hot outside, I was shivering. Maybe this would be the day we would hear Papa's voice.

I thought about the day of my first communion and how I stood on Papa's shoes during a dance in the town square. The lights twinkled, and I felt like a princess. Papa whispered in my ear, "You will always be my perfect little girl." I remembered how Mama glowed watching us, her hands cupping the light bump of her belly—my future sister.

But Mama miscarried. Sadness moved into the

orchard and gobbled up whatever we had left until Papa had to leave for Texas.

I didn't want to be a victim anymore. I wanted to be in charge of my life. I realized I hadn't heard the voice in my head in a long time. Was that a good or bad thing? I stared at the jewelry store across the street.

The telephone booth ate our coins hungrily. I pressed my ear against the receiver to listen as Mama spoke.

"*Buenas tardes*. My name is Aurora. I am looking for my husband, Arturo. He is a worker from Cedula, Mexico. Do you know him? Is he there?" asked Mama.

"We haven't seen him in a while. Sorry," said the voice.

Mama hung up the phone.

No one had seen him.

I hate the telephone.

CHAPTER 28
Metro

The sound of distant bells haunted me. Flora hadn't come by in a week, and I was worried. Perhaps I could light a candle for her and Papa today. "Can we go to Mass?"

Mama rubbed her neck and stretched her fingers. "I'm still tired, maybe we should rest more." She was still sniffling from the phone call on Saturday night.

Every morning I had been doing errands for Jorge, I explored a little farther into our neighborhood.

"But I wanted to show you a shoe store across the street from the market. The church is on the way and we haven't been to confession in years. It's time to go. It would make Grandma happy," I said to Mama.

I also worried that no one would show up with food for Mr. Mann. Someone needed to feed that crazy man.

"Nora, we don't have money or time for any of that. No shoes. No clothing. No confession," answered Mama.

I wiggled my toes so that they seemed extra long in my brown *huaraches*. "I need new sandals. I wanted to light a candle for Papa."

What I really wanted was that calm feeling in a quiet place. Not the muffled voices of a television I couldn't watch blaring from a wall.

"We have to do something. Let's go downtown. To the tall buildings." I put the postcard in my pocket in case we found Papa. I could show him how I carried it everywhere to think of him. "Maybe we could even stop by the shoe store? Payless. Isn't that a pretty word?" Perhaps if I stood at the back door of Payless, someone would throw out a pair of expired shoes, just like the nail polish.

At the market, I bought the bus tokens and two

doughnuts for Mr. Mann.

Mama was in the produce aisle holding a grape-fruit. "These are no better than what we had in our orchard," Mama said. "We could have sold our grapefruit here and none of this would have ever happened."

I hugged her. "But now we know, and we can tell Grandma to send all of our grapefruit right here to this market."

I crossed the street to Mr. Mann. When I put out the bag, he crumpled his eyebrows. "Jorge doesn't make donuts."

"I know," I replied. "M-A-N-N."

A small smile creased into the filth on his face. "Thanks, Tessa." I had found that when you spelled his name it made him happy.

Bus 212 arrived. We sat in the center of the bus as it rumbled down the street. I watched the streets roll by. We crossed under a huge highway and the tall buildings sprang to life in the front window. They shone in the morning sunlight and almost looked like tall soldiers with gleaming badges of mirrored windows.

"Let's get off here," I said. "Maybe we can find a construction site."

The buildings stretched to the sky in front of us. I bent my head all the way back just to see the top. The buildings shaded the sun and the concrete sweltered around us.

I imagined that during the week women in fancy suits wore high heels, making them as tall as the men. Men wore suits and ties in dark colors and shined shoes. Perfume, lipstick, briefcases.

Maybe one day, I could be one of these people. When I was better educated. When I had shoes that fit.

"We need to find Canal Street. That's where men go to look for work," I said.

"How did you find out about Canal Street?" asked Mama.

"I asked, and all the men say that's the place to go."

The buildings began to fade, and soon there were no more fancy shops, and I couldn't read the signs. We walked under a large freeway.

Across an empty lot, several groups of men stood alongside the road. I squinted to see the name on the sign: CANAL.

In Spanish, *canal* means a big place of water. It can also mean a trough. I didn't know what it meant in English. It looked like a dead end.

"This is the street. Let's go talk to some people," I suggested.

A truck stopped at the corner, and suddenly all of the groups burst into action, screaming at the truck.

"I've got a team of eight! Ten dollars an hour!"

"His team is all drunk. Choose us. Nine dollars an hour."

One man pushed the other, and soon they fought in the dirt.

Three other men approached the truck. Mama and I looked through the crowd for Papa. I couldn't see him anywhere.

A white man in a cowboy hat stuck his head out of the pickup truck. "I need ten men. The first ten into the truck come with me. I only need diggers today."

The men poured in, each scrambling for a seat in the back. The smallest one was pushed off to the side so that an older man could get on. He threw a clod of dirt.

All of this happened in less than a minute. Mama grabbed my hand. "He's not there. Let's go."

"Someone has to know him," I said with a strangle in my voice. The hair on the back of my neck stood up and tingled. Grandma said tingles were a sign of bad things. She always told me to be aware of the signs. I looked up. No birds.

Men sauntered back to the shade and pulled out brown bags.

"*¡Hola, mami!*" one of the men shouted. It wasn't a compliment.

Mama stopped in her tracks, flinching.

"Let's go," she pleaded under her breath. "He's not here. Papa wouldn't want us to be here."

"*¿Cuanto?*" screamed another man.

How much? Why was this man asking "how much"? Mama began to step backward.

"Has anyone seen Arturo Mirales from Cedula, Mexico?" I yelled from our spot across the lot. I wasn't leaving without information.

"I've got something for you to see." The man pointed at his pants. Mama's nails dug into my palm.

"Arturo Mirales from Cedula, Mexico. We haven't heard from him in a long time. We need to find him." I tried to sound as adult as possible. *Pretend it's easy until it is.*

"Come here and I'll give you something." I could smell the alcohol from across the parking lot.

We turned and ran.

"I think we should go home now," said Mama with a sigh.

We were finally at the bus stop. "It won't be long. At least the bus will be air-conditioned."

"No, I mean home to Mexico. Home," she said softly.

"We can't. Not without Papa."

"But maybe he's already on his way. Maybe he's at home waiting for us," Mama said in an unsure voice.

"We'll find him!" I screamed, stopping in the middle of the sidewalk. "We're here, and we're staying. We just need to try harder."

Mama shook her head. "But what else can we do?"

"I don't know," I said. "But Papa promised me we would be together."

Mama wiped another tear from her eye. "*Mija*, I know. . . ."

"No! A promise is a promise. We're staying."

I could go to school. I could have friends and a real life. It was a plan.

We boarded the bus and sat on opposite sides of the aisle all the way back to Quitman Street.

The bus finally squeaked to a stop. The squealing brakes reminded me of the creaking branches from our orchard.

Mr. Mann sat on his corner, face frozen and shoulders hunched. What was his plan? Is that what happened when everything went wrong?

Where was God for him?

Or for us?

CHAPTER 29
No More

Late in the afternoon, Keisha appeared with a pair of plastic shoes that matched hers. "Hey, guess what! I made these for you; now we can be shoe twins."

They were purple sandals with sparkles and pom-poms glued to the plastic thong. Ugly and horrible, they fit perfectly. I grabbed her tightly. "Thank you, my shoe twin."

Keisha loved to correct my accent. "Not 'chew,' 'sh-ewww.' These are called flip-flops, but I don't know how to say that in Mexican," she said playfully.

"I made these in VBS. This is a prototype. That's a fancy word for the first kind of shoe you make. I'm gonna practice making more with a hot-glue gun and stuff I got from the craft store with these coupons. But we can't wear these to school, because I don't want anyone to steal my idea before I can get on one of those TV design shows."

"School?" I asked. My mind ran fast to catch up with her words.

"I can't believe that we have to go back to school so soon. This year we have to have a uniform. We get vouchers."

"Voucher." It came out sounding like "boucher."

"Yeah, most of us around here get vouchers 'cause none of us can afford that kind of stuff. Now that I think about it, I bet you gonna get a voucher. You gotta get some kicks for gym class. You can't go around barefoot, and no flip-flops at school."

Keisha had a way of pointing out the painfully obvious. "I wouldn't even be going to schools in this neighborhood except for my mom works here. She prefers we stay—you know, in other places."

"Where live?" I asked.

"We live over on the other side of I-10. Houston freeways are a big belt, keeping us all cinched up in different parts of its body. Nobody wants their belly touching their butt."

I didn't exactly understand, but I let Keisha talk. "I'll be at the high school in two years. Do you think we'll still be friends then? I bet they figure out your English ain't the best and take you to ESL."

"School is where?"

"Aren't you registered? Now, which grade are you in?"

The conversation grew more intense. How was I to explain that I didn't know what grade I should be in? She asked that question a lot. Usually I pretended I didn't understand.

"ESL?" How long would it take for her to figure out my game? I felt like I could trust her, but Mama told me never to tell about our status.

"You know, so that you can learn English. English as a Second Language. I bet you were in that class last year but you didn't know it. That's why it's so important that I do this design stuff. I can't spend my life being a dummy. You neither."

If Keisha had confidence about getting ahead in the world, I could too.

Keisha jumped off the side of the pool and kicked her legs up in the air to make a big splash. Just then, a girl in short shorts with a massive tattoo on her leg got soaked from the wave.

"*¡Eres majadero! ¡Idiota!*" Water drenched her tight white shirt. She made such a scene, everyone turned their head. "*¡Moreno!*"

"Sorry, I didn't see you." Keisha's brave behavior shrank in the shadow of the shrieking girl.

"You shouldn't even be at this pool!"

"I said I'm sorry." Hurt spread across Keisha's face.

"Stop," I called to the shrieking girl. I felt myself pulling up to the ledge so I could look her in the eye. Her heavy makeup stained her eyes. Was this the girl who pushed me on the first day? She had a star tattoo—the kind that wasn't finished on Flora's hand.

"What did you say to me?" She took a step closer to me with her fists clenched.

I was not a victim.

I climbed out of the water and straightened my shoulders and stood toe-to-toe with her. "Stop it. Stop!" I took another step, and she stumbled backward into the grass. Anger pushed me forward.

Keisha yelled at me from the water. "No! Not one of the Chulo girls!"

My insides felt like exploding. Someone had to

stand up. Someone had to do something. Keisha had protected me before, and now it was my turn to stand up for her.

I felt the words hissing out of my mouth. "I want better! *¡No mas!*" Anger welled inside my fists until I couldn't control them any longer. As she lunged at me, I pulled back and punched her hard in the mouth.

Lauren blew her whistle from the chair. Jorge came barging toward the pool.

Blood smeared across my hand. The Chulo girl pounced like a cat, but I moved and she hit the concrete. I kicked with my bare feet and grabbed at her gelled hair. Her neck pulled taut, but she was no match for my fury.

I heard Flora scream from the fence. "Leave Nora alone. She's with me!"

I pulled at the girl's hair while she screamed. I dragged her to the edge and pushed her into the pool.

"No, Tessa! No!" Jorge screamed, jerking me back by my arm.

The wet girl stared at Keisha, and then took a long look at me. I crossed my arms and cocked my head.

I glared back at Jorge. "I'm not Tessa!" Grandma always said to choose your fights. I had chosen mine.

The girl climbed out of the pool with her hand

pressed up against her lip. She flipped a middle finger at me and jerked her body at mine, a threat to continue to fight.

Flora rushed to my side. "Are you okay? I'll get this taken care of."

Jorge pulled harder on my arm. "Get back to the stand!"

"Where have you been?" I asked Flora harshly.

Keisha stood wide-eyed. "You have got to be careful with those people."

Jorge yelled at Flora, "And stay away from us! You are nothing but trouble."

I called out to all of them, "She didn't do anything!" Flora slunk away from the pool.

But Jorge continued to pull at my arm, blind with rage.

Keisha trotted after us. "You said it all in English. Where'd you learn how to do that? Have you been holding out on me?"

I shrugged my shoulders because I didn't know how the words came out. Something boiled in my stomach and the words wanted to flow like lava.

Keisha pulled me into a hug and her braids fell into my hands as I squeezed her back. The last person who had squeezed me that tight was Grandma.

"Not a whole lotta Mexican folk would stand up for a black girl."

Jorge barked, "Keisha, call your mother and go home. Don't come back for a while. It's not safe."

Keisha interrupted, "But Flora said—"

"Go. Now." He turned to me. "Don't pick fights with gangs!"

The afternoon dragged on like the minutes before Christmas. Jorge slammed his paperwork around and glared at me. There was no conversation, not even the droll of the radio. Just his fury.

His anger was about Tessa, and I was just her replacement.

It seemed everyone here was mad about something.

Chapter 30
Brave

At five, Jorge told me to take the rest of the day off. I worried he would fire me in the morning.

I wandered the streets until I found a church; at least, that's what I thought it was. It was a metal building with a cross on the sign. I wore my new purple shoes, which seemed completely wrong in a church.

"Hello?" I called out as I stepped through the door. The nuns told me the church was always open, but no one said anything about knocking.

"*¿Hola?*" I called out again. My voice echoed against the cold metal walls.

In Cedula, we had wooden pews made by people in our town. Women brought candles; men cut down trees to make an altar. The merchants pooled money to buy a few beautiful statues of Mary, Jesus, and Guadalupe. All in an abandoned store.

I didn't see any of that here. There was a piano and metal chairs. There was a stand at the front. No candles burning. An empty wooden cross. No Jesus. Maybe they had taken him off the cross to wash him? Maybe that's why no one was there.

I took a seat in the back and looked at the altar. Why did it seem so long since I had prayed? I couldn't even remember how long we had been in Houston.

I whispered, "Dear God. I hope You're here some-where. Please help me find Papa. Please don't let me be fired." I paused, thinking about the multi-tude of all my other sins. "Please forgive me for the fight."

But maybe I could find a better job. Or maybe, this was a sign that instead of working, I should be going to school.

The church told us to pray about what we were

171

thankful for. We were supposed to say thankful things too.

"Please bless Mama and Grandma. Thank you for Keisha and Flora. And these horrible shoes." For good measure, in case He wasn't listening before, I said it again: "Please help us find Papa."

I worried I was supposed to be praying in English. Did God speak different languages in different places? I used the most important English words I knew. "Papa. Mama. School. Job. Please."

I felt like I was a pleading child, begging for candy. Like the beggar in Matamoras. Where was my mercy? No voice whispered in my head. I was here alone.

After I left the church, I walked toward the school Keisha described. It had a high fence around the yard, but I found a gate and could peek into the windows.

Books lined every shelf. There were more than twenty desks in each room. Chalkboards stretched behind the front desk. Three computers. Pencils, pens, art supplies. There was more in this room than what had been bought in three years by the nuns. I felt like I was staring into an oasis of education.

The fight had been a sign. I was supposed to be

going to school. Perhaps this was my birthday present from God. An opportunity. But where was the voice to guide me?

A woman in jeans opened the door and walked into the room. She had long brown hair, a pencil woven through it to keep it away from her eyes. She carried a plastic bin. I ducked out of view and continued down the street.

I silently wished Flora would appear so I could get answers to all of my questions. We never had any time to really talk. And I wanted to ask her how she was doing in school. And did she get to have a *quinceañera*? And had a boy ever kissed her? And what happened to her father?

And, and, and.

I just wanted a friend I could really talk to—like sisters doing hair, doing nails, and sharing secrets. Like my unborn sister, who disappeared from my mother's belly and floated away with the rain.

But the sun dipped lower in the sky, and I knew it was time.

At home, Mama sat at the table with her arms crossed and a fiery look on her face. "I can't believe you almost cost us our jobs! You're lucky Jorge wants you back in the morning."

I sat out on the stoop weaving until a few stars strained to sparkle in the city sky. I was waiting for Papa like a lost dog that didn't even know her owner's name anymore. I was just someone else who couldn't go home. Not yet. Maybe not even ever, because home didn't exist for me without him.

CHAPTER 31
Punishment

Jorge made me pay for the fight in sweat even though the pool was almost completely deserted. I'm sure if Jorge could have told me to pick up every grain of dirt in the park, he would have. It was like he couldn't put enough space between us.

No one talked to me for three days. Manuela wouldn't even take the small basket I had painted with green polish. The more hurt I felt, the angrier I became. It was like the world had turned its back on me.

On day three, Keisha came around. "Can she talk to me now?"

Jorge shook his head. "No. Go back to the pool."

Keisha stood straighter than I had ever seen before. "She was just doing the right thing and y'all shouldn't punish her for that."

Jorge barked back, "She doesn't need to be involved with any of those Chulo girls. You know what kind of problems we had with Tessa."

Keisha pulled herself up tall. "Nora was just defending me."

Jorge barked, "Is that true, Nora?"

I leaned against the broom. *"Sí."*

"Why didn't you say so?" Jorge's eyes softened. "It looked like you were picking the fight, especially with Flora hanging around."

I shrugged my shoulders. He never gave me the chance to explain. I chose the fight because it was the right thing to do.

Keisha held her hand over her heart. "She wasn't. I promise. I'll even look out for her when we go to school, and Flora ain't hanging around those people. She's at the library; I saw her. She looks real upset."

Jorge pursed his lips. "Nora, go on your break." He

scratched at his head and used his fingers to trace the lines of his jaws.

Keisha peeked over the counter. "Where are the shoes I gave you?"

Jorge laughed. "Those are the ugliest shoes I have ever seen."

I put them on with pride. "Chew twins."

I sat in the shade with Keisha, but she was too quiet. "I try go church," I said.

"Girl, there's lots of church around. What kinda flavor are you?"

I pointed to both of us. "Church. School. Go."

"Huh? You and me? Vacation Bible School is all finished, and we're mostly black at my church. I mean, you could come if you want—but don't get all scared when people whoop and holler to praise the Lord in my church. We know how to call on Jesus."

I nodded like I understood her words, like this was all normal. "I go school. You help. *Mañana*. Chew twin."

Tomorrow would be my fifteenth birthday. Even though she was younger, I wanted Keisha to help me get into school.

Keisha started backing up. "Nope, sorry. I once ran around the neighborhood and my momma switched me so bad. I learned my lesson. I stay at the pool or the library." She paused. "And now that you've pissed *them* off, ain't no way we going running around. Don't be on the streets by yourself, 'cause it just makes you an easy target. We can still be shoe twins—here at the pool."

Jorge pointed at his watch and called me back to the stand. "I gotta get to the bank." My break was over. From the look on his face and the tone of his voice, it seemed the punishment was over too. There was no apology. I didn't need it.

Lauren waved from her stand for a drink. An idea popped into my head. As I entered the pool, Lauren stuck out her hand for the drink like I was doing her a favor. She didn't care about anything except her cold free drink. As I came closer to her chair, I felt a new feeling. I opened the lid and waited for her to look at me.

As her blue eyes peered down, I poured the lemonade into the grass.

"No mas," I said.

Lauren's mouth gaped open.

"No more free for you. Learn manners."

Keisha gave me a thumbs-up. I believed in my own courage.

* * *

At home, Mama grinned from ear to ear. "Guess what!"

I hadn't seen her smile like that in a long time.

"Jorge just brought this over. He also told me how he made a terrible mistake about your argument at the pool. I did too. I'm very proud of you for defending your friend, but next time, let's not make it into a brawl. Okay?"

I leaned in to her. Her approval meant more than any apology.

"And you are so smart to have someone mail a letter! Concrete Guy also gave me the name of a place to call to find Papa," she said proudly. "You read it for us, my lucky star."

I grabbed at the letter from Grandma. Apparently, even God understood my Spanglish. This was an early birthday present.

Inside, I swear I could smell Grandma's hands, and maybe the slightest scent of grapefruit.

Dear Aurora and Nora,
I miss both of you so much that I think my heart
is breaking more each day. Even the grapefruit
are in mourning because there is no little monkey
climbing their trees. The tax man has come twice,

179

and things look very bad. I gave him some of my
special candles, but they buy very little time.

My bright spot is Hector. He brings your
telegraphs and watches Mass with me. We pray for
you. Be safe so that one day we can be together
again.
I love you,
Isabel

The few simple words broke my heart. The tax man was on his third trip, which is very bad news. Then what? We wouldn't have anything to return to. Grandma was too old to be smuggled up in a truck like Mama and me.

I wiped away my sweat and sadness. "At least we have a phone number. Did Concrete Guy say anything else? Maybe we can figure something out."

"No. We'll call tonight," said Mama. Her eyes were wrinkled with concern.

But my mind thought about the telephone and how it never gave the answers I wanted.

And neither one of us mentioned my birthday tomorrow.

CHAPTER 32
The Truth About Tall Buildings

My thoughts remained on Grandma. She would tell me when I was worried, "Let the wind carry your worries away. That's why God makes a breeze in the morning."

But the still, humid air of Houston sat on me like a *gordita* waiting for the buffet. Out on the street corner, I noticed two small children walking home with their mother pushing a shopping cart. The kids carried shiny new backpacks. I knew this was another sign.

"School starts soon. I need supplies," I said to

Mama. I figured if I said it like it was something we were supposed to do, she just might follow along.

Mama looked at me funny. "You need real papers to go to school."

"We'll just buy them." It seemed you could buy anything in America for the right price.

"No, I wish we could. First we find your father, send money home to Grandma, and then you go to school."

"But—"

She shook her head. "School takes time away from work. Grandma needs us to send more money."

"But—"

"Or we might lose the farm."

"But—" I tried again.

Mama cut me off midsentence. "I want to send you to school too, but not yet."

"I've been praying at a church nearby," I said. I had seen a priest only once. He waved at me, but I pretended to be deep in prayer, so he let me sit in peace.

"I don't think God can answer every prayer we ask for," said Mama sadly.

The empty church had become my place. No screaming from the pool, no television blaring through the wall, no mother trying to tell me what to do. Heck, even God was silent. I prayed in the empty church because they had air-conditioning. In the cool air, I could pray for hours. I even left a bowl on the altar.

Mama pulled out a napkin stained with salsa. "This man says he worked with your father in the spring. He described the tall buildings. I think this is the right number."

I frowned at my clothes. "Keisha talked about a voucher. Do you think we could get a voucher? I feel like I'm starting to look like Mr. Mann."

Mama stared at my feet. "We just don't have extra money. You want clothes, or to help Grandma? Which do you choose?"

I didn't want to choose. I put on the sandals and followed Mama to the pay phone outside of the market. I didn't even try to listen anymore. I flopped down on the bench meant for the bus people. No one was waiting for the Metro. My empty earlobes ached when I looked at the jewelry store across the street.

This was my opportunity to stare at the window of Payless. How I wanted a pair of brightly colored sneakers. Maybe I could tell Manuela it was my birthday and she would buy me a pair. The idea of a *quinceañera* was a distant memory. Just a pair of shoes. My family. School. My list always seemed to be growing. It would have been easier if I didn't want anything.

Mama slipped coins into the phone. "Hello. My name is Aurora. I'm looking for my husband, Arturo, from Cedula. He stayed at your mission with a man named Luis. Do you know where I can find him?"

I dreamed of what it would be like to wear a new uniform to my first day of real American school. I could sit next to Flora and have a fresh notebook with light blue lines. A teacher would point at the board, and for once, I would begin to learn everything I really needed to know. Papa would be so proud of me.

I would be smarter when we found him. I could put my education to work and save our farm. I could even open a store and sell things from Cedula.

Mama grew quiet. It seemed every noise from the street silenced around us. Even the crickets stopped their nightly screaming from the trees.

"No," they would say. "We don't know him." That would be it.

Mama shook. "No. No. I don't understand."

There was more frantic talk. I tuned in to the conversation.

Mama continued to babble, shaking her head no.

"Maybe it was someone else? Maybe you are mistaken. This couldn't be true. You're wrong."

I couldn't understand what was happening. Mama grew pale.

"We came from Mexico to find him. He is everything to us. Please!"

Mama dropped the phone and held her hands to her face. I could see the tears dripping between her fingers. The cord dangled in the air.

I picked up the phone and heard a voice.

"Hello? Could you repeat what you just said?" I asked.

"*Está muerto*. He's dead."

CHAPTER 33
A Cruel Joke

Mama's mouth hung open as the tears washed down her face. She melted to the ground.

"Get up," I said. "Right now."

Mama bent over with her hands on the pavement.

"Mama, pull yourself together. We can't act like this on the street." I noticed a car full of girls rolling by for the second time. I worried it would be a carload of Chulo girls.

Mama rocked back and forth on the pavement. Over and over again she muttered, "No." Brake lights

186

flashed in the twilight.

I wanted to get out of the street. People were looking. She had finally lost her mind because of someone's cruel joke.

"Mama, come on, it was a mistake. We can find out later. No one knows us here. Maybe this person is a *mentiroso*. Come on, we're leaving." I didn't know what was true. A car with dark windows stopped. Fear crept into my stomach, because I couldn't fight off a gang of vicious girls. "Mama, time to go. Now," I whispered into her ear, trying a nicer tone.

I pulled Mama's shoulders until she looked up. "Maybe it isn't true," I said with hope. I needed a fresh breeze to blow our worries away, but the night stood still.

Flora's face appeared in the window. "What's going on? Get in before those girls come by and cap you in the head."

Mama cried out, "He's dead! He's dead!" She clutched Flora's arm.

She tried to pull back, but Mama pulled harder. "Who's dead?" Flora asked, her tone softening. "Who?"

"Mama, please," I snapped back. I had to get her off the street, but she collapsed into a ball on the concrete.

"No, no, *señora*." Flora spoke with a tenderness I had never seen. "Please, let me take you home."

I hovered over my mother. "She starting saying crazy things. You have a car?" I asked Flora.

Anger and concern mixed on her face. She rubbed my mother on the back. "Please, let me give you a ride home. Let me help you the way your daughter helps me."

The scream was like a wild dog. "My husband. Her father," Mama wailed and pushed me away. "What will we do? *¡Dios!*"

My throat was closing. None of this was real. "Mama, it's *not true*."

Flora held my mother's arm. "Come on and stand up."

Mama's wailing turned into hiccups. She muttered Papa's name over and over, snot pouring down her face.

"I just need to get her home. She's getting worse after each phone call."

"Look, take the help and be quiet," Flora said as we walked toward the car. "Omigod, what are those shoes you are wearing?"

"I like them." My brain was numb as I pulled Mama into the front seat.

Flora drove us in silence except for Mama's hiccups. At our door, she helped Mama in, but came no farther. "I gotta go, because I didn't ask to borrow the car, and it's not like I have a license. My brother will probably kick my butt if he finds out." She disappeared into the darkness without even a good-bye.

I sat on the stoop waiting for the joke to end. Flies buzzed past my ears into the screen door, sounding like miniature cars zooming on a freeway.

"Nora!" my mother wailed. "Don't you understand? Your father is dead!"

I clapped my hands over my ears and screamed. "We are not victims!"

In front of me stood a lone shadow. Mr. Mann. Without eye contact, he put a bag at my feet and shuffled away.

The receipt waved in the evening breeze. Doughnuts.

It was nine thirty. We hadn't eaten, so I cut up leftover sandwiches from the stand and a few of the pastries. Mama turned toward the wall when I brought her a plate.

I had to convince Mama the phone call was a mean joke. "Come on, Mama. Please eat something.

Tomorrow we will try again. *Mañana* we can find a new number to call. We'll find Papa. It can't be true."

Once again, I wasn't sure if we could find him, but I wasn't giving up. Mr. Mann's doughnuts sat on the table.

I closed my hands in prayer. "Please, God. I'll do anything."

I imagined my entire life. How I was supposed to have a father and a mother. Live in an orchard in Mexico. Have a beautiful *quinceañera*. Graduate from a school and be smart. Marry a nice boy. I was supposed to fix all of this.

Gone. Finished. It couldn't be. I wouldn't let it.

I climbed into bed and held my mother, trying to close the sorrowful space between us.

CHAPTER 34
A Smell in the Air

I woke up with Mama's arms around me. My T-shirt was wet from all of the crying. The clock read 7:30 a.m.

"Mama, wake up. We're late for work."

Mama groaned. It sounded the same way as when we were in the truck: low, monotone, and sad. It almost sounded like Mr. Mann spelling his name.

"Mama. We'll get in trouble." Mama rolled over in the bed toward the wall.

Jorge's truck was parked at the stand. Customers

191

were already lined up. I grabbed my clothes and ran out the door. I didn't have time to mother Mama today.

I pulled on my stained apron. "*Señor* Jorge. My mother is sick today and can't work."

He growled as several customers walked out of the line. "Why? She didn't act sick yesterday. Manuela and I are supposed to get our permits today." He shook his head. "We can't depend on anyone. I knew things were going too good to be true."

My voice cracked as I said it. "Please don't be mad at us, but something happened last night." I burst into tears with the rush of last night's memory. "Someone said Papa was dead."

Jorge dropped the tortilla from his hand. "What?"

"I don't know . . . nothing is making sense." I could feel fast breaths coming out of my mouth, but no air could get into my lungs. The world spun in slow, lazy circles.

"*Niña*, what's happening?"

I crumbled to the floor of the stand. "He stopped sending telegrams, so we came to find him. We were asking the workers who were coming for food. Last night, someone told us he died."

The words came out of my mouth faster than I could think. It felt like the water flowing in the pool. The words splashed out because it just now seemed true.

Jorge shooed away the customers in line. "Sorry, everybody. Closed for the morning." He grabbed napkins and wiped the tears from my face. I was crying so hard that I could no longer hold in the sobs while my entire body shook.

"Calm down, it will be okay," said Jorge.

I couldn't imagine anything being okay. We left everything to find Papa, but now almost everything was gone, including him. I was beginning to believe the phone call. Maybe he was dead.

Jorge took my hand. "Okay, let me lock things up and we'll go to your house."

"No. It's just a mistake. I'll work today, and then Mama and I can continue to look for Papa." I didn't want to be fired. Someone had to work.

"I'm trying to help. No one will starve if we close the stand for one day. Let's go home and talk to your Mama," said Jorge.

We walked across the park as I sucked my breath in and out for air. Jorge's cross twinkled in the sunshine of the morning. His burly arm around my shoulders felt familiar. The way I fit under the crook of his arm, it just made my heart ache even more.

The shadows of the trees had just begun their long walk across the park.

Jorge called through the door. "Aurora, I'm coming in. Nora told me what happened."

Mama twisted in the bed, away from Jorge and the light.

"Tell me what happened, Aurora. Maybe I can help. You could have told us what was going on. You know we understand about these things," said Jorge.

Mama turned over to look at us. Her eyes were so swollen from the crying you couldn't see the brown of her eyes. "They told me he had been killed in a construction accident. They don't even know what happened. They said one day he just never came back for his things."

"Who is this? How did you call them?" asked Jorge.

"I found someone who knew him. They gave me this." Mama held up the stained napkin, now wet with tears.

"Give me the number so I can call them. Maybe we can get an explanation. Do you have family I can call?"

I interrupted. "My grandmother lives in Cedula. She doesn't know about all of this." My heart ached

194

for Grandma. "We're illegals. Don't call the police."

Mama pointed to the table where we had collected all of the numbers. "We've called so many people. Where is Arturo?"

Jorge flipped open his cell phone. Then he got into his truck and drove away. I climbed back into bed with Mama and closed my eyes. I held her tight. My job today would be to cling to what we had left.

Each other.

Chapter 35
Mr. Bubble

In the afternoon, Manuela showed up at the door with several bags. She came inside and wrapped her arms around me. She remained quiet as she unpacked the food and prepared dinner.

The smell of chicken enchiladas filled the room. Manuela walked into the bathroom and filled the tub. I saw a pink plastic bottle, and suddenly the tub filled with bubbles. "Come on, girl, it's time to wash some of this sadness away. Jump in."

The water was hot and soothing. If I closed my

eyes, I could feel Grandma's touch. From the kitchen, warm smells tried to replace the sadness in the room. I could have wrapped the feeling around myself for days, breathing in the scent of safe and comfortable.

A new towel appeared over my shoulders. It felt thick and scratchy as I dried myself off. Manuela combed my hair in silence. "Just like Tessa."

I had heard the name so many times. It was like a ghost floating in and out of the park. "Are you finally going to talk about her?"

"Tessa was my niece."

"I know that part. Where is she now?"

"She disappeared. She might even be dead. Gang initiation, problems at home. I grew very close to her when she started having problems with her mother, but it wasn't enough."

Silence. What could I say?

"No one ever went to jail. No one talks about it, and I find myself looking for her everywhere," said Manuela.

"I know how you feel." I felt the sorrow of her grief. I wondered if I would be doing the same thing. Papa had died, but it didn't hurt like it was supposed to, because I had been mourning him for so long.

Manuela shook her head. "But today isn't about

197

my loss. We have to concentrate on you. You are here. Tessa is not, and she'll probably never come back."

Out in the kitchen, Mama rummaged through the other bags. She had finally gotten out of bed.

Manuela left me in the bathroom. She hugged Mama tightly. "I'm sorry. *Lo siento*. Maybe now we can help?"

Mama's tears welled up again as she leaned in to Manuela's soft shoulder. "*Gracias*. But I don't know what to do—he's gone."

I didn't either. Even though I was clean and the kitchen was full of warm smells, the faint aroma of garbage was still in the air.

Outside, Mr. Mann put another bag of doughnuts on our stoop. He also laid a braided string cross next to it.

CHAPTER 36
Free Fall

Mama looked so sad that her eyes were dragging on the floor. She barely moved inside the house.

I was stuck somewhere in between. Should I just give in and cry, or should I do something to prove all of this wrong? Maybe this is what I deserved?

Papa couldn't be dead. How could he be dead if we had come all this way?

Jorge knocked at the door, *"Hola."* He spoke in a low voice. It was the way my papa had talked to birds with broken wings as he placed them back into their nests.

Manuela waved him in. Mama looked out the window, tears in her eyes.

"Thank you for everything. I don't know what to do. Where do I start? How do I even find the body?" said Mama.

The body. The name of it was horrible. Papa was not a body. He was a real person—flesh and blood.

"No, don't worry about that right now," said Jorge. "I'm not sure how to tell you the news."

I sensed Jorge knew something we didn't know.

"What do you mean?" asked Mama.

"I mean, I'm not sure that you are ready to hear about what happened," said Jorge.

I was tired of not knowing. Papa had been gone for so long; I needed to know just so I could feel something for him, to shake off this numbing cold that was taking over my body.

"I want to know," I said. It was easier to pretend to be strong than to wilt in the corner. I had built a brick wall around myself and I clung to it for support.

Jorge looked at me. "No, I'm sorry; you are too young for this. Why don't you take a walk or something?"

I was furious and felt like hitting something again. "Too young? You mean I'm too young to think I'm going to die on the back of a truck, or to take care of my mother, or to earn money for my family?"

Manuela approached me. "I know you're upset, but—"

I didn't want her pity, either, so I lashed out in whatever way I knew how. "I'm not Tessa, and no amount of babying me will make it better that she disappeared!"

Manuela held her face like she had just been slapped. "You know she disappeared after the gang thing. She dealt drugs. We couldn't even have a funeral. Not even a good-bye."

"My father didn't do any of those things! He was just a worker and he didn't do anything wrong! Where is my good-bye?" Jorge's and Manuela's eyes grew large with horror as I screamed my version of the truth.

But shouting wasn't enough to quell my anger. "I know I'm here in America, where everything is supposed to be better. But it isn't. I want to live in a place that doesn't smell like garbage. I want my *quinceañera*. I want to be fifteen again."

Mama had covered her eyes and tears dripped onto the table from between her hands.

"I want to know," I said. "It's what I have left."

201

"The truth won't make this easier," said Jorge.

My mother finally raised her head. "Please, we both deserve to know."

Jorge let out a large sigh. "I spoke to the family Arturo stayed with for a few weeks. Apparently, he fell from a large building where they didn't have much safety equipment. Several of the men who stayed in the area saw the accident. They think the company dumped him by the work hall."

Mama turned white. "They dumped him? Dead?"

"The company worried the construction site would be shut down because of the illegals. All of the other men left the site because they were afraid. The owner threatened that he would turn them in to Immigration," said Jorge.

¿La migra? Is this why no one would talk?

Jorge continued, "The family who was renting a room to Arturo says that all of the men have left the area. She didn't even know which work site. It's just a rumor to her."

A rumor. Then this story might not be true. Papa *could* be alive.

"But where is my husband? Did they bury him?" asked Mama.

I felt my feet starting to burn. The earth began to

shake, preparing to swallow me.

"The woman said she wasn't sure if the story was true. But I called the city morgue. If it's him, he's buried nearby."

Buried. Buried. No.

"How could this happen? Is it really him?" asked Mama.

At any moment, I would be gobbled up. I felt like a piece of glass, falling from the counter, shattering on the tile.

"The local police never did much of an investigation. This story is all over the work halls, because the men told me the same version. Every few months, a body is dumped there. The workers think it's the companies. The police think it's drug dealers. This happens every day. It's not even news. I'm so sorry."

There was hope. Dear God, please don't let Papa be dead. "So maybe Papa isn't—"

"I'm sorry. The woman at the mission gave me this. She said it was with his things."

It was a Western Union receipt with the word "Cedula" written on it. It was wrapped around a small picture of Mama, Grandma, and me.

CHAPTER 37
Frozen

It was true. Papa had only one picture of us. He would never leave it behind.

Angels did let things fall from the sky. "What have we done to deserve this?" I said to the ceiling, as if God might answer me.

On one hand, a huge weight of my expectation had been lifted. Here was the answer. Papa wasn't a promise breaker. But a huge sadness crept into my shoes and was crawling up my legs like a hairy spider. I couldn't move, or the monster would bite with its poisonous wrath.

Papa. Gone. Papa. Gone.

I felt Jorge lift me from the chair and place me into bed. I remember Manuela brushing my hair with her fingers. I didn't have the energy to fight.

Time twisted in hazy circles. Was it afternoon? Had months gone by?

"Tell me about Cedula," I heard Manuela ask.

My lips were moving, but it wasn't me talking. Someone else's voice knew how to answer the questions.

"We lived in an orchard with grapefruit. My grandmother has owned it for more than twenty years. My papa was born there," I said.

"That sounds nice. Where is your grandmother now?" asked Manuela.

"In Cedula, waiting for Papa. We send her money from Western Union. We wanted her to come and be here when we found Papa."

"I see. Do you have a phone in Cedula?"

"No, we lived outside the town. I know Hector has a phone in his office."

"Who is Hector? How come I've never heard of him?"

"Oh, he runs the bank. We became friends because I went there every week."

I felt her fingers rubbing small circles into my

back. Grandma would do this whenever I couldn't sleep, her gentle patting lulling me to sleep.

"How did you come?" I asked her.

"Oh, sweetie, I didn't come to the States, I was born here. My grandmother came across a long time ago."

"Tell me the story," I said as I closed my eyes.

She murmured the way Grandma used to whisper to me. "She came like lots of people: through the river. She lived with Jorge and me for five years before she died. Would you like to see a picture of her?"

Manuela opened her purse and brought out a color picture. The woman had white silvery hair like Grandma, and deep brown eyes. She could have been Grandma's twin sister.

"Manuela, she looks like my grandma Isabel." I realized that I didn't even have a picture of Grandma. I had been carrying her around in my head.

I missed everything about my grandmother and her silly grapefruit recipes. It seemed all fruit made me sad or nauseous since the mango incident.

"Manuela, would you look for Flora? I would really like to see her," I asked.

"Sure, honey. Just get some rest," she answered.

My eyes closed. I dreamed of sweet-smelling trees and fingers combing through my hair.

Chapter 38
Unmarked

I woke up to Mama's clanking in the kitchen. Fresh doughnuts sat on the table.

I forced myself to sit up. "Mama, why didn't you wake me? We'll be late."

Work had been engraved into my head. No work. No money. No nothing.

"No. Jorge and Manuela are taking a few days to get everything ready for the new restaurant. I think they went to Nuevo Laredo to buy tables and chairs."

"So what do we do for money?" I asked.

"Jorge left us some. He told me not to worry, just to rest."

I didn't want to rest. I wanted to see Papa's grave.

"Mama, did Jorge tell you where Papa was?"

Mama stared at the sink. "Yes. It's up the road a bit. We can go by bus."

I tried to ask for directions to the cemetery from someone who didn't speak Spanish. The black woman in the shop sneered at us. "I don't speak none of that Spanish, so you'll just have to find someone to translate. You should learn to speak English. This is *America*!"

We bought flowers at the market. The loud, playful music seemed all wrong today. Once again, we were in a place that was all wrong for us.

The bus wouldn't come for an hour, so we waited in the park. There was no sign of Flora, and I wondered if she had disappeared out of my life too.

Mama pushed me on the swings. I wished I could swing high enough to fly away to Mexico, but my wings never sprouted.

I spun Mama around on the merry-go-round. I saw her frown over and over again. The swimming pool was closed for cleaning, and the heat was exhausting.

As we boarded the bus, I realized I would never

have another birthday with my father. I wanted to make myself stop loving him, because maybe then the pain would go away.

When we found the cemetery, we had to ask directions from a groundskeeper. After walking deep into a quiet area, we saw the headstones change from marble to flat stones of concrete.

"I'm not sure which one he is," said the groundskeeper, pointing to a flat area that had recently sprouted small blades of grass. We sat in the full sun until our backs burned and mixed sweat with our tears.

Papa's grave didn't even have his name. I kissed the ground and left my leather sandals with him. They didn't fit me anymore. I wanted to give Papa something of myself.

Mama didn't notice my bare feet. I guess she didn't have anything left either.

"I love you, Papa," I whispered.

And we walked back to Quitman Street.

CHAPTER 39
Spitting and Stealing

Two days later, resting grew old and boring. Mama continued to lie in the bed, but I felt like a caged tiger.

I walked to the cemetery. It was a long hike on a bumpy, cracked sidewalk overgrown with weeds. I didn't mention to Mama where I was going and I left my purple flip-flops under the bed.

She was lying facedown on the mattress crying when I left. We hadn't moved from the apartment in two days. I was suffocating in the misery. I wanted Keisha or Flora, because I could talk to them in ways

I could never talk to Mama. I was ready to open my mouth and let it all spill out.

Jorge and Manuela weren't home from Nuevo Laredo yet. Time stood still in this sticky, sad place.

Large trucks zoomed by on my walk. They were going too fast for this street. The sidewalks sloped toward the curb, and I could feel the hot rush of wind as the trucks passed by. Gravel smacked my legs and bare feet. Ants I passed seemed to slow down under the sun's constant glare. My head was hot.

But who cared? I did.

Freshly cut grass bloomed in the air. I could hear the busy freeway beyond the trees. I could see the black iron fence running down the road to the left. On top of the gate was a white concrete angel looking at me with sad eyes.

"This isn't It," I muttered to her.

At the back of the cemetery lay lots of little stones. I wasn't sure which one I was looking for. I hoped something would look familiar, and my sandals would be the markers. I passed hundreds of gravesites with fancy marble stones, small trees, or benches. Poems and names were written on the side, but I wasn't interested in collecting the sad words of dead people.

At the back of the cemetery, hundreds of tiny headstones lay sprinkled in the grass like stones in the street. Nothing looked familiar. I walked down several rows, and when I was sure no one was looking, I stole a few flowers from different graves.

"I'm sorry," I whispered to the headstones. "I'm sure you don't mind sharing with someone who died with nothing." I had now turned into a thief.

The words scared me. Papa died with nothing. He died alone. Those people threw him away like trash.

There were no names on the stones. A small chapel stood in the back. Maybe this was a good time to rest. Maybe this would be a good time to pray.

The door of the chapel was locked. No one was around, so I sat on the steps for a while with the flowers wilting in my hands. The shade of the tree let sunlight dance through them and make hazy pictures on the concrete. After sitting for a few minutes, I realized how tired I was.

I stood up and tried the door again. I needed it to be open. "Hello? Is anyone there?" I called.

The thorns from the stolen roses pierced my hands, so I threw them down to the ground. My palms throbbed in pain.

212

No one answered the door and I didn't care how much my hands hurt. "Where are you? Open up! I need you. I need to talk to you." I beat on the door. "Why did you throw him away? Why have you left me here all alone?"

The wind blew through the trees in a gentle rhythm.

I needed answers, and God wasn't giving me any.

Angels don't come out of the sky. They hide inside locked churches.

"I hate you. Do you hear me? I hate you!"

I took the postcard out of my pocket and tore it to shreds. Bits of paper fluttered away in the summer breeze.

I spit on the steps of the church and walked home.

CHAPTER 40
Qué Onda Guero

I felt the booming of the bass, the high triplet of a whistle. I didn't pay attention.

"Hey, Tessa. Where are your shoes?" A teardrop was tattooed into the corner of his eye and a star on the crook of his hand.

"*¿Qué?*" I turned my head to see a suave-looking man hanging out the window of a black Monte Carlo.

"I haven't seen you in a long time. Get in; I'll give you a ride."

Tejano music sang from the car. I had to pick up

214

my feet in a fast dance to keep them from burning on the concrete. I shook my head no and continued to the corner.

"Come on, Tessa, we could have a little party." He pulled the car around, blocking me from crossing the street. "Like last time."

There was another teenager in the car. I could see his shiny hair as he opened the car door. "We didn't know you was back in town. Let's *rumba* like last time." He pulled at my arm.

"No," I said, shaking my head. "You're confused; I'm not her."

The driver leaned over to show me an ID card from his visor. "Sure it is. Here's your picture. It was my prize, but I never thought you would be brave enough to show your face around here."

I leaned in. It was a Texas driver's license with what looked like my picture, but the name said Contessa Ana Villareal. I reached for it when I felt them pull me into the car.

"Come on, *chica*. It was so much fun last time, but we never got to finish." The oily-headed boy slid in next to me and closed the door. The driver moved his hand up my leg.

My brain defrosted and a voice filled my head.

Get out of the car.

I hit his hand away, but he dug his fingers into my thigh. "What, you don't like it no more? You loved it last time."

Last time?

I heard the voice again.

Get out. Escape. Survive.

I pulled the gearshift as hard as I could, and we all jerked backward violently. I punched at the horn. My feet kicked at the other boy, but it seemed I could only reach the dashboard.

The voice grew louder.

Run.

The driver lashed at my face. I kicked again and the car lurched up and over to the side. I was now on the floorboard. The left side of the car was jacked into the air.

Hydraulics—the car was jumping in different directions. An automotive tango was making us into passenger popcorn.

Fuerte. Be strong.

I was tangled into the passenger's legs, but I couldn't reach the door handle. His ankles held me down into the alcohol-soaked floorboard.

Fight. I suddenly realized this was not a voice of

216

a patron saint. Today it was my father's voice. *Fight!*

I sunk my teeth into his Achilles' heel and kicked with all my might. The car lurched again. The horn blared. Curse words bounced in the car in a blur.

I reached the handle, and fell out of the car.

The giant anthill boiled in front of me. I reached down and scooped.

Small red dots engulfed my hands as I threw the dirt into the Monte Carlo. I scooped again and again. Throwing. Cursing.

"You won't do to me what you did to her!" I screamed.

More ants. More swearing. Until the car sped away.

I heard howls in the distance. I could see them slapping at themselves as the car turned the corner.

I smacked the ants off my hands, arms, and feet. Angry welts rose on my arms and legs.

At my feet lay Tessa's ID card.

I picked it up and ran the rest of the way home.

CHAPTER 41
Bonfire

A bonfire of pain shot from my arms and legs from the ant bites.

I stopped on the stoop to scratch. A pink candle glowed on the doorstep. It smelled terrible.

I worried about the fight with the boys. Would I be in trouble again without anyone asking me what had happened, or would Tessa's ID redeem me? I wiped my face and discovered my nose was bleeding. Jorge's truck sat on the curb.

I looked down at my shirt. Footprints. Blood. Dirt.

How could I explain any of this?

The door to the apartment opened and the scent of a familiar soap hit me square in the face. "*¡Dios santos!* What has America done to you?" screamed Grandma.

I couldn't believe my eyes. "Am I dreaming?" I asked, rubbing my eyes and reaching out to touch her.

Grandma grabbed my arm. "What happened? Aurora, get some rags and olive oil."

I stuttered, "I-I was at the cemetery visiting Papa. There were these boys . . ."

"Did they attack you?" Jorge stood defensively. "Do you know who they are?"

Everyone's questions flew at me at the same time. I scratched at my legs, wanting to claw them off. The fire ant bites seemed to sting all the way through my skin down to my bones.

"They thought I was Tessa," I said.

The room grew instantly quiet.

I flipped the ID card onto the table. "They had this."

The rush of the moment caught up with me. Like the panic couldn't run as fast as I could and had finally huffed into the room. I didn't want to think about what the boys wanted from me and I didn't want to think about what they took from Tessa.

Manuela grabbed at the plastic card. Her palm covered her open mouth.

"Grandma, how did you get here?" I asked.

Manuela began to cry. "We have to call the police. Nora has to tell them what happened."

"No!" Mama and I shouted.

"Police?" asked Grandma. "Won't they send us back? We can't go back. I just got here."

Jorge held up his hands. "We'll sort this out later. Everybody calm down."

"B-but—" stammered Manuela, "I need to know."

I clapped my hands over my ears. It sounded like cats fighting outside the window late at night. Garbling, high-pitched nonsense.

Jorge put his hand on Manuela's shoulder. "This isn't the answer. It's just a piece of plastic. This doesn't bring Tessa back. Perhaps it's time you let her go."

"B-but—" she stuttered again.

Jorge pulled her toward the door. "We need to go. The appointment for the permit is in ten minutes." Manuela dabbed her eyes and loudly blew her nose.

"No police," I said. "Please!"

Jorge motioned his finger for me to come closer. "I'm not calling the police. I'm the one who smuggled your grandmother in, so now is not the time to get the authorities involved," he whispered.

Outside the door, Mr. Mann stood with a worried look on his face, doughnut bag in hand.

CHAPTER 42
Telenovelas

Mama filled the bathtub with hot water and a bit of bleach. I sat in it until my skin wrinkled and the itching stopped. Grandma sat on the toilet seat while I bathed.

"Have they told you?" I asked.

Her eyes misted. "I know, *mija*. Jorge told me. It's why I came."

It was easy to let the wall down around my heart if I had somewhere soft to land. "But why? Why did he have to die?" I sobbed. With Grandma, I could be who I really was. Naked or not, my emotions were out for all to see. I unleashed my heartache like a hurricane on Grandma.

She held out the dry towel and pulled me into an embrace. "How could I not come? There is nothing for me to wait for in Cedula," said Grandma.

"We were coming home to you and the orchard," I said. "I was going to fix this for us."

Grandma's strong shoulders slumped. "There is no more orchard. Or at least, none that we own, and you are not responsible for fixing anything."

I pulled on clean clothes but my shoulders ached. "I could have tried harder."

Grandma pinched her nose in thought. "No. It was taxes, fertilizer, and the lack of money. None of it was from your lack of trying."

Grandma seemed older, her wrinkles deeper. I felt like it had been years since I had seen her rather than months.

"But Grandma, it's been in our family for years."

Grandma's chin cocked stubbornly in the air. "And now it will belong to a new family."

So much heartache. First Papa. Now the farm.

Grandma wiped the tears from my cheeks. "*Mija*, I choose you. I choose to be here and make a new life with you." It seemed her positive spirit had survived the trip.

"You're going to stay?" I asked.

"Yes, of course I'm staying. You are my family. You have fixed me."

"But how?" I asked.

Grandma smiled cunningly. "A friend loaned me the money to get to Nuevo Laredo to meet with Jorge and Manuela. He knows I will return the favor."

"Who?" I asked, holding my breath, waiting for the answer.

"Hector," she said.

"My friend Hector?"

"No, *mija*. He is *our* friend Hector."

CHAPTER 43
Lost and Found

Later that day, I awoke to the bickering in the kitchen between Grandma and Mama. It seemed like some things didn't change.

"Tell me everything. Exactly," said Grandma.

"I only know when they buried him. Who knows how they do things here in America?" said Mama testily. The dark circles hollowed under her eyes.

"But we must seek justice and give honor to Arturo," she insisted.

"You don't think I want that?"

225

I could tell Mama felt insulted. What did Grandma think we were doing here in America—eating cake? None of this was easy.

Mama stared into her coffee. "But they threw him in the street like dirty dishwater. He died alone."

"At least a funeral service at a church," demanded Grandma. "We can do that much."

Funerals cost money—more than we had. If there was a God, He didn't like us. Why would I bother giving our hard-earned money to Him?

"But Isabel, we are illegal immigrants, we can't call attention to ourselves," said Mama. "You need to learn that we can't go stomping around here demanding things."

"God will care for us," said Grandma.

A burning in my stomach rose like boiling milk as I sat up in the bed. "We don't even count as people here."

Grandma reached out to me. "*Mija*, you can't deny God and His plan. You of all people should know. God told you to come here."

Panic and pain had finally caught their breath. They were ready to chase me with all of their might. I bellowed out my thoughts, even though I knew it would hurt Grandma's feelings. "There is no God and

He has no will. When will either of you face reality?" I hit the door as hard as I could as I ran toward the park. "Because nothing matters anymore."

Maybe I could outrun these feelings crashing all around me.

My feet pounded the pavement. *I hate you,* I thought spitefully as I headed toward the park. I could feel the heat from the day soaking through the soles of my feet.

In the park all I wanted to do was climb a tree, but the limbs weren't low enough for me. I needed to be up in the air, away from all of this. I jumped and reached for any limb, but even in my desperation, nothing would come close. I grasped for anything. Even the trees were against me.

The pool was closed. I tried to squeeze between the bars, but my body wouldn't budge. I wanted to dive into the cold water and to hold my breath and never come up. I wanted my father, who would never be coming home. I wanted away from this place called America.

I cried for myself until the tears turned into salty rivers at my feet. Nothing here would make things better. The suffering was all for nothing. There would be no party, no school, no Papa, no nothing.

I thought I heard the trees whispering in the Gulf breeze.

Go home. Go home.

But where was home? Could it really be here? Mama and Grandma—did that make a home?

I didn't want to hear voices anymore.

And where was God? None of the lessons the nuns taught said anything about this. Wasn't He supposed to protect us? Wasn't He supposed to listen to my prayers? I wondered if God or faith even existed on Quitman Street.

The night was busy transforming itself. Fireflies danced from one tree to another. Mosquitoes bit my legs, and frogs from the bayou sang songs only they understood.

Mr. Mann appeared from behind a tree. "Go home, Nora. Go home."

I shrugged my shoulders. "But where is home?"

He looked at me with his dark eyes and tattered face. "Over there." He pointed. He dropped one of my bowls in my lap. "Dreams in there." He shuffled away.

Perhaps he wasn't crazy.

What seemed like hours later, I heard my name in the dark. It was Mama.

"Nora! Nora! Please, I can't lose you, too. Nora!"

228

I would not give away my dreams. I ran toward her in the night, because I wanted to be found. I wanted someone to rescue me.

I ran past the trees and the swimming pool and into her arms. The moon was full. The shadows touched us as we stood in the middle of the park, hugging each other.

Mama pulled me into her strong arms "We can start over. We may not matter to America, but we are important to each other," Mama whispered into my neck.

I didn't answer. I felt like a flat tire—out of ideas on how to make this work. Tomorrow I would think of something new.

CHAPTER 44
Sweet and Sour

I woke in the morning to the smell of hot coffee and eggs. There was a feast on the table and I saw *magdalenas* on the table. "I'm sorry for how I acted last night. I'm glad you're here. I've missed you."

Grandma sat next to me, pouring the coffee and sugar like it was falling out of the sky. "I've missed you too. I think you have been carrying the world on your shoulders. Maybe with me here, it will be easier."

Things couldn't get any harder. "Where's Mama?"

"She went to work, but Manuela left money for shoes. Some girl named Flora came by last night. She said she'd come by later."

I raised my eyebrows. "What did she want?"

Grandma fluttered in the kitchen. "Not much; she just said she was your friend and wanted to check on you. I didn't want to say anything about the fight. You can tell her yourself if you want."

I took another bite of eggs. I wondered if Flora was at home, wherever that was.

"Now, what are those purple shoes?" Grandma was busy with a basket at the counter. She chattered like she didn't need a response.

"I should take my candles to the market because I've seen the bugs here. These candles killed several cockroaches on the porch last night. Jorge says they even keep the mosquitoes away from the stand."

I couldn't help but laugh at her antics. "Grandma, those candles stink to high heaven."

A smile cracked through the sadness on my face. It felt like the first fruit you pull from a grapefruit tree in the fall. Hard to wait for and tough to pull—but you're so happy when it finally comes down and you taste the first bite. Sweet, then immediately sour, then sweet again.

231

"Yes, and that is why they are useful. I plan to earn my keep here in America."

The heavy load I had been bearing seemed to ease up a bit. "So we really are staying? No more Mexico?"

Grandma looked a bit sad, but she straightened her shoulders with hope. "Perhaps my candles will make us millionaires. Then we can just buy citizenship and visit Mexico whenever we want."

I had a feeling it wouldn't be like that, and perhaps it was time to develop new hopes. For the first time, the apartment didn't really smell like garbage, perhaps a bit cleaner. I was ready for shoes and clothing that fit. "Grandma, if it were that easy, everyone would be doing it."

We walked the neighborhood. I felt protected with her by my side. On the way past the thrift shop, we passed the metal church.

Grandma pulled on my hand. "Show me the building." She had sold five candles and two of my bowls— which she now called dream bowls. It's like she had a secret sense of who would buy in the neighborhood.

I didn't want to go inside. "No, let's wait until later." I didn't want to have the God conversation again so soon.

Grandma pulled open the door. "Is this the church your Mama tells me about? Perhaps we should go in just for a second?"

The church was having a small service. Usually it was empty during the week, but today clumps of people sat in the pews. A woman was singing. Her voice floated all around the metal building like a gentle wind. We slipped into the back row. Grandma crossed herself before we sat down. My hands were frozen at my sides.

In the front was a coffin—a funeral. Incense permeated the air. I had never really been to a funeral, but once, in Cedula, I peeked into a church when one was going on.

The coffin was shiny and black with silver hinges. It looked like a piece of jewelry. The flowers surrounding it fought with the incense to leave a trace of perfume. When the song was finished, the priest stood over the coffin and sang. "El señor, *tiene misericordia.*"

I anxiously shifted in my seat, awaiting the lightning that would strike me down. How do you tell your overly religious grandmother that you have committed the worst sin of cursing God?

"Shhhh . . . God will understand you here,"

Grandma whispered. "He always has something to say, whether we are listening or not."

A black priest sang from behind the altar. He sang first in English, and then in Spanish. He raised his arms, and the congregation repeated his song. "Lord, release my wants. Release my fears, and let me come to You," he cantered.

Despite my anger, I found myself mouthing the words, in both languages.

CHAPTER 45
All Good Things

"How was your exploring this morning?" asked Mama when we returned to the stand for lunch.

Grandma beamed. Her candle basket was empty and her wallet was full. All but one bowl had sold. "Very good. We went to the church. Do you know when they have confession?" I asked.

I felt lighter. Happier.

Manuela answered, "If you want to do it in Spanish, Pastor Michael will do it late on Wednesday for those who are from the Catholic tradition. They have

235

another pastor, but we like him the best."

"Is he the black priest who sings?" I asked.

Her face looked puffy, but her eyes weren't as sad. "Yes, he's Honduran. He says a Mass on Saturday evenings in Spanish. The metal building is just temporary until the new church is built. I'll introduce you if you want."

I had never imagined a black person knowing Spanish. I just assumed you had to be brown. I didn't even know that differences in religions and color made no difference.

Manuela grasped my hand. "Thank you for giving me Tessa's card."

I never thought about keeping the card, but it would have made my life simpler. Since I resembled a younger version of Tessa, it would be easy to pretend I wasn't illegal. "No problem." I scrambled for the words. I had made it this far, and I could go further and still be a good person.

"Flora came by and spoke to me. I gave her some breakfast and discussed which boys had probably attacked you. We can still call the police if you want," said Manuela.

"No. I think I showed them that I wouldn't play their games," I said, looking at the scabs on my legs.

"But I worry about Flora."

"She seems like a decent person, just very alone," said Mama.

"She's just trying to get by," I said to both of them. "It's not her fault about her family."

Grandma touched my hair slightly. "It's not your fault about Papa. Forgiveness will come in time, but anger will only make us bitter. You did everything you could."

I didn't want to be angry forever, but I wasn't quite ready to absolve the world of my problems. The passion of the anger kept moving me forward. I still wanted more.

"Thank you for helping us. For Grandma. For . . . for everything." Without them, we might have just wasted away in the street. Maybe we did count as somebody.

Manuela wiped her brow. "Will you work for us in the restaurant?"

Mama and Grandma were already nodding their head.

I had another idea. "If you don't have a name for the restaurant, I have a suggestion."

CHAPTER 46
Saying It Out Loud

Four days of hard work rolled by in Jorge's new restaurant. Grandma cleaned floors and counters. I folded menus, polished the used chairs and tables, and scrubbed corners. A stink candle sat outside the back door. A neon sign blinked outside the front.

CONTESSA

Grandma wanted to go back to the church. Without a television, she missed nightly Mass.

I wondered if Hector bought the television, too. I said a silent prayer for our friendship.

Even though guilt plagued me about the ugly things I said to God, I didn't mind going. I wanted to see the priest who sang at the funeral.

"*Niña*, wear something clean, please," said Grandma, "and not the purple shoes."

"Grandma," I said, rolling my eyes, "I'm not six years old. I know the proper way to dress." But I put the flip-flops on anyway.

Grandma pinched my cheek playfully. "You will always be a little girl to me."

I knew what I was going to wear. I'd hid the dress all summer. When I slipped it over my body, I realized it was shorter. It used to touch the bottom of my knees.

Grandma didn't notice the small flowered blood-stain that sat right over my heart. A small altar of candles sat humbly in the corner, and I lit two. I should have deposited some money, but I'm sure God understood I was a little broke right now. Besides, what I was praying for was courage. God could keep silent, but what I needed was enough strength to open my mouth.

Grandma came out of the confessional looking satisfied.

"How did it go?" I asked.

"Very well. He is a nice priest. It's the same one from the funeral a few weeks ago. Do you want to go in also?" she asked.

I entered the small booth and the door slid open. I was worried my heart would jump out of my chest and land with a splat on the floor.

"Yes, my child," said Father Michael.

"Forgive me, Father, as I have many things to confess."

"Go ahead."

"Father, I haven't been to confession since . . . I don't know. I've cursed God. I've lost my faith."

"Why did you curse God?"

"I cursed Him because He let my father die. I cursed Him for all of the bad things that have happened. I feel He has abandoned me."

"Your father died?"

"It wasn't long ago. We came here to find him. I prayed really hard and God didn't listen to me."

"Do you think God didn't listen to you because your father died?"

"I'm not sure. But I have a question. Can I ask you?"

"Well, this time is reserved for the confession of sins. Why don't we finish and then you can ask me questions."

240

"Yes, Father. I'm mostly finished." I could have confessed for hours, but I think I covered the big stuff.

"Child, your sins are forgiven. Pray to God to restore your faith. Look for Jesus in your everyday life. Say the Lord's Prayer, and know God forgives those who ask to be forgiven. I will pray for you."

He shut the window. I peeked out of the booth. No one else was in line. I moved into the pew and waited for Father Michael.

I wasn't exactly sure if I had my faith back. I wasn't sure if I was finished being mad at God. I wasn't even sure if God was finished being mad at me.

Grandma knelt against the altar. Several more candles had been lit, including a pink stinky one. She was deep in prayer.

"Those are some big thoughts for someone as young as you," said Father Michael as he sat next to me. His skin was the color of warm flan. His voice made me feel comfortable, and my heart stopped beating so hard.

"I'm not legal. I don't have any papers." I could feel the bloodstain on my dress burning. I didn't know if that was a good thing or not.

"God doesn't care about your status. He wants you to have faith."

I sat in silence. So many questions I wanted to ask,

but Father Michael said what I needed to hear.

"And like your own father, he wants you to have hope. You have not been abandoned."

He patted me on the back and I sat in silence for a while. It didn't matter about the voice anymore, because I think I had found my own.

As I turned around, I saw Flora sitting in the shadows. "Where have you been?" I asked in a loud whisper.

"Hiding. The police have been in and out of my house lately. My brother's been arrested. I've been staying with a cousin across town. If I'm not home, I don't have to watch."

"Sorry about that," I said. "My dad died. I mean he was dumped or killed or something."

Flora bunched up her lips. "Yeah, I know. I'm sorry. What are you going to do?"

I shrugged my shoulders. "Not sure. Survive."

Flora nodded with knowing. "Yep, you gotta make your own way."

"Yeah, I think I can. I mean, I'm almost sure I can," I said with more confidence. "But if things get too bad for you at home, why don't you come to my place?"

"We'll see," said Flora. "That's a lot of people for one bed. But, your grandmother is nice. It'd be good to be around a family who cares. She was feeding me just like you did."

"You can be my family, Flora. No matter where you are, you can belong to us."

Flora's eyes moistened. She gripped me close and then disappeared out the doors before I saw Grandma rise from her place.

When Grandma and I exited the church, I saw Mr. Mann sitting on his corner. He never asked people for charity, but I knew what he needed.

I went back inside and made a sign on an old church bulletin.

I MATTER.

—MR. MANN

Chapter 47
Pronunciation

I didn't pause at the door of the school. I pushed it open and walked up to the desk.

"I like to school," I said in halting English. Grandma stood behind me, huffing and puffing from the two-block hustle.

The woman nodded her head and her wide braids brushed against her cheek. She opened a filing cabinet and handed me a stack of papers. On her feet was a pair of neon pink flip-flops. They had bells, crosses, and a black Jesus glued to the plastic part of the thong.

"Do you need a pen?" she asked. I nodded my head yes, but I couldn't take my eyes off the shoes.

She rattled off so many words at once. "I'll need a copy of your ID, a Social Security number, proof of residency, a copy of your mother's driver's license, and your last school report card so we can get the records." Her nails were long and painted with tiny curlicues.

My heart sank. I didn't have any of these things— just fake papers. "I no have." I shook my head.

Her eyes were soft and familiar. "Honey, how old are you?"

What should I say? I didn't have anything left but the truth. "*Quince*. I'm fifteen."

"Where do you live? Are you in this district?"

"Quitman. By the park." I pulled out Mama's fake work papers and her Mexican voter registration card. This was as much as I had.

Grandma pulled on my arm, whispering, *"Vámanos. No es importante. No hoy."*

"No," I whispered back at her. "It is important. I need to do this."

Keisha came around the corner slurping from a carton of milk. "Nora! Where have you been?"

It felt like the cool breeze coming off the top of the grapefruit trees.

245

"Is this your swimming-pool friend?" the woman with the braids asked. I knew why she seemed so familiar. Keisha was a younger, slimmer version of her mother.

A warm, comforting feeling surrounded the room. "Yes, yes!" I said.

Keisha chattered excitedly. "Yeah, Mom. She's not in my grade, but we're gonna sit next to each other at lunch. See, she's wearing my shoes. I think I'm gonna design them and become rich."

I answered with a chuckle. "Yes. Chew twin."

Keisha sauntered over and began writing for me. "Hey, Mama, don't you have that migrant worker paperwork? She hasn't been in the district that long. She's like one of those traveling Mexicans, but the good kind."

Her mother handed me a green form. "Will you need the reduced lunch program?"

Keisha nodded. "Mom, she needs all that stuff. Where can we get her vouchers for supplies?"

My father's spirit filled my heart. "*Bouchers*. Yes. *Lonche*." I knew it wasn't exactly how to say those words, but it didn't exactly matter. I had some hope. Perhaps it could grow if I planted enough seeds.

Grandma clutched her purse with wide eyes. I

pulled her away from the door and introduced her.
"Keisha, *mi abuela*."

Grandma smiled, but I could see her shaking as she extended her hand to my friend.

"We live in Texas now," I said, patting Grandma on the back. "We stay."

I wondered if I should write Hector a letter to tell him our new address, off Quitman Street.

Epilogue
Next Year

My watch blinked 4:00 p.m. I tied my apron around my waist and hurried toward Contessa's. My homework wasn't finished, and today was a long shift.

This morning, I skipped first period and put a few flowers on Papa's grave. One year ago, on my fifteenth birthday, we found him. His death. My womanhood.

The humidity from the day steamed around us. The sound of a distant lawnmower sang along with the chorus of morning traffic. I wished so desperately to hear Papa's voice. A separation of six feet might as well be a million miles.

Occasionally, I found solace in the fact that we were close to him, trying to achieve a better life. But grief is a snake. It climbs into bed with you and occasionally bites you on the toes, filling you with poison.

The smell of the pink candles glowed outside the restaurant on the patio. They do keep the bugs and bad spirits away. Mr. Mann knighted himself their protector because he liked to light them if any of their flames went out. He rarely talked, except for the spelling, and his shopping cart is parked by the back door each evening because the Salvation Army won't let him bring it in. We have the cleanest alley on Quitman Street.

I hope we can buy a real tombstone for Papa one day. I spend less of my time thinking about Cedula, and more on my homework.

My eyes barely had time to adjust to the cool interior of the restaurant. "Happy Birthday!" Mama, Grandma, Keisha, Jorge, and Manuela shouted.

A large pink cake with rose flowers. Manuela pinned a deep red rose corsage to my white shirt. A small bag of doughnuts sat by the cake.

Keisha placed a small tiara over my ponytail.

"I know you've always wanted one, so I designed this one special from the craft store. Maybe you could wear it to the prom next year?"

Flora came rushing into the restaurant, tying her apron. She held a small package of lipstick. "It's red. A real woman should wear red lipstick." She paused. "And something on her ears." She held out a pair of dangling earrings. I smiled at her, knowing that her stealing days had stopped when she began working for Jorge.

"A sweet sixteen party for my American girl." Mama kissed me gently on the cheek and handed me a box.

Grandma clasped her hands under her chin. Her smile spread across her entire face. "*Mija*, open the present."

I ripped open the white tissue. Inside the small box was a gold necklace.

A small cross with a green stone. A medallion of Our Lady of Guadalupe.

"The Guadalupe is from me," said Grandma, "because of your faith and courage."

"I had the peridot put in the cross. It's your birthstone. It came from Mexico to remind you where we came from. The jeweler said this stone can protect you from negative things in the world."

Mama smiled but sadness radiated from her eyes. "The cross was Papa's."

I held it in my hand and closed my eyes. I could barely remember his face. It had been almost five years since I had seen him. But I remember the feeling of being in his arms. Protected.

And then I remembered the way the cross would dangle out of his shirt.

I opened my eyes and looked down at the gold cross. It matched my memory.

I quickly pulled the chain around my neck. I opened the lipstick and smeared a little on my lips. I knew this was just the beginning of all the things I would do.

In the reflection of the mirror, I saw the tall buildings of downtown Houston and saw what my father's hands had made.

I heard the rustle of the trees and knew there was something more.

He's here.

He's all around me.

Finally, we're all together.

❧ GLOSSARY ❧

abuela — grandmother

aspirina y aceite — aspirin and oil

baño — bathroom

Banco de Nada — Bank of Nothing

Bollios, ten *para un* dollar — Hard rolls, ten for a dollar

Buen provecho — Have a good meal

cabrito — baby goat

calma — be calm

Calmate, calmate. — You calm down, you.

cartas — deck of cards

Cazar de Apestar — stink candle

Cazar de Espectro — spirit candle

cerrado — closed

¿Chica? ¿Donde está su Mama? — Girl? Where is your mother?

chimenea — chimney

chupacabra — the boogeyman

¿Cómo estas? — How are you?

coyote — human smuggler (slang)

cucarachas — cockroaches

¿cuanto? — how much?

decisiónes — decisions

despacio — slowly

Dios — God

¡Dios Santo! — Dear God!

dos minutos — two minutes

Ella es mi amiga. — She is my friend.

elotes — corncobs

Eres majadero. — You're annoying.

escuela — school

¡Estaba tratando de matarnos! — It was trying to kill us!

Fabuloso — a heavily scented cleanser popular throughout Latin America

familia — family

frío — cold

fuerte — strong

fútbol — soccer ball

galleta — cookie

gordita — fat lady (slang)

ha muerto — died

¿Hambre? — Hungry?

Hola, mami. — Hey, sweet lady.

huaraches — sandals

Iglesia de Guadalupe — Church of Guadalupe, the patron saint of Mexico

jabón — soap

jefe — boss

la iglesia — church

la luz — light

la migra — immigration (slang)

la voz — voice

ladillas — an STD similar to gonorrhea (slang)

lechita — milk (slang)

Lo siento. — I'm sorry.

los lentes — eyeglasses

mañana — tomorrow

magdalenas — a Mexican pastry

mas pesos — more money, more pesos

mensajes — messages

mentiroso — liar

mija — Contraction of *mi hija*; "my daughter" (slang). Also used as an endearment.

morenos — black people (slang)

mota — marijuana (slang)

los Negros — African-Americans

¿Niña, tienes servilletas? — Girl, do you have napkins?

¡Niños! ¡Cuidado! — Be careful, kids.

No entiendo. — I don't understand.

No hablo Inglés. — I don't speak English.

no mas — no more

no mas dinero — no more money

no para — don't give

No problema. — No problem.

Nos estamos yendo. — We're leaving.

para siempre — forever

pueblo — tiny town

puta — prostitute

Qué onda guero — a reference to a song by Beck, meaning "What's up, dude?" (slang)

¿Qué más? — What else?

¿Quieres algo? — Would you like something?

¡Que terrible! — How terrible!

quince — a small tiara worn in the hair

quinceañera — the fifteenth birthday and celebration; a rite of passage

rumba — dancing party, not necessarily the specific dance

sangre — blood

taquería — small restaurant

Te amo. — I love you.

Tejano — Texan and Mexican fusion music

tetas — breasts (slang)

tía — aunt

Tiene misencordia. — Have mercy.

tipo de cambio — exchange rates

torta — sandwich

Un minuto, por favor. — Just a minute, please.

Vámanos. No es importante. No hoy. — Let's go. It's not important. Not today.

velas malolientes — stinky, smelly candles

via — the way

washatería — a Laundromat

Acknowledgments

I am grateful and blessed to have found my agent, Blair Hewes. Thank you for loving Nora and always standing in my corner.

Thank you to my editor, Katherine Tegen, for taking a chance on me and making this process so easy after eight years of no. And to Jennifer Christie, your detailed attention helped every nook and cranny shine. Thank you to the countless and nameless people who will touch, support, and love this book at HarperCollins.

It's not really fair that only my name goes on this book, because I have been nurtured in so many ways. Thank you to Julie, Sally, and Risa—you made Dallas home. Thank you to Jenny, Mary Ann, and Joyce— you made creative Sunday afternoons over tea and cookies at the yellow house magical. My promise to you is that you never have to read this book again.

Thank you to Thaddeus Bauer for the letter that saved this novel—otherwise it might be in the trash.

Shout-outs to the organizations that have let me hang out by the watercooler: The Blueboarders, SCBWI, the Elevensies, and 2KII.

To all my friends from JLP and The Next Chapter who always ask, "When is that book coming out?"

And to the employees, families, and customers of Fiesta Mart—thank you for sharing your lives and stories. I am humbled.

Last, but not least, my husband, Tom, and my son, Allen. You keep me centered in my insanity and always ask, "What's for dinner?"